W9-BZT-762

Praise for *The Forgers*

"*The Forgers* is quintessential Bradford Morrow. Brilliantly written as a suspense novel, lethally enthralling to read, and filled with arcane, fascinating information—in this case, the rarefied world of high-level literary forgery." —Joyce Carol Oates

"Bradford Morrow is, quite skillfully, paying homage to one of Agatha Christie's most famous whodunits. Yet even then, he offers a few twists of his own and will keep all but the most astute mystery aficionado guessing about the truth until the end." —*Washington Post*

"Bradford Morrow's *The Forgers* is a bibliophile's dream, an existential thriller set in the world of rare book collecting that is also a powerfully moving exposé of the forger's dangerous skill: What happens when you lie so well that you lose touch with what is real? In beautifully controlled prose, Morrow traces the shaky line between paranoia and gut intuition, memory and self-delusive fiction, hollow and real love. It's perfect all-night flashlight reading—Bradford Morrow at his lyrical, surprising, suspenseful, genre-bending best."
—Karen Russell, author of *Vampires in the Lemon Grove* and *Swamplandia!*

"Bradford Morrow illuminates the seamy side of the rare-book trade in *The Forgers*." —*Vanity Fair*

"In *The Forgers*, Bradford Morrow hits the sweet spot at the juncture of genre crime fiction and the mainstream novel with an almost mystical perfection. Readers of either form will be gratified and impressed, and those who are readers of both will be thrilled. In its deep knowledge of books and those who trade in them, and in its thousand vivid, unexpected turns of phrase—its depth of both subject and language—*The Forgers* could have been written only by Morrow and at only the rare and striking level of mastery he has now achieved."

—Peter Straub, author of *A Dark Matter* and *Ghost Story*

"With *The Forgers*, Bradford Morrow has masterfully combined an exquisitely thickening plot, an informed appreciation of the antiquarian book world, and a deep understanding of what makes the obsessive people who inhabit this quirky community do the sort of impassioned things they sometimes do, up to and including the commission of horrific crimes. Morrow has hit the ball out of the park—*The Forgers* is a grand slam, in the bottom of the ninth, to boot. This is a bibliomystery you will want to inhale in one sitting."

—Nicholas Basbanes, author of *A Gentle Madness* and *On Paper*

"[An] artfully limned suspense novel . . . The insights Morrow offers into the lure of collecting, the rush of forgery as a potentially creative act, and underlying questions of authenticity render the whodunit one of the lesser mysteries of this sly puzzler."

—*Publishers Weekly* (starred review)

"*The Forgers* . . . stuns from its first line . . . Morrow offers a suspenseful plot that coexists with gritty characters and ominous imagery." —*Fine Books Magazine*

"*The Forgers* is a reader's dream: intelligently written, with beautiful details paid to the use of inks and stationary, pen pressures and hand flourishes. Bradford Morrow has created in Will a character rich in criminal indignation."   —Bookreporter

"Morrow writes with a sure, clear voice, and his prose is lush and detailed . . . Recommended for readers who enjoy atmospheric literary thrillers such as Caleb Carr's *The Alienist*."   —*Library Journal*

"Will, the narrator of Morrow's seventh novel, is a fine creation . . . A pleasurable study of the lives of book dealers."   —*Kirkus Reviews*

"So well written, *The Forgers* will take some time to finish as readers might want to reread every sentence."
                    —Jean-Paul Adriaansen, Water Street Books,
                                        Indie Next selection

THE
FORGERS

ALSO BY BRADFORD MORROW

The Uninnocent
The Diviner's Tale
Ariel's Crossing
Giovanni's Gift
Trinity Fields
The Almanac Branch
Come Sunday

BRADFORD MORROW

THE FORGERS

The Mysterious Press
New York

Copyright © 2014 by Bradford Morrow

All rights reserved. No part of this book may be reproduced in any form or by any electronic or mechanical means, including information storage and retrieval systems, without permission in writing from the publisher, except by a reviewer, who may quote brief passages in a review. Scanning, uploading, and electronic distribution of this book or the facilitation of such without the permission of the publisher is prohibited. Please purchase only authorized electronic editions, and do not participate in or encourage electronic piracy of copyrighted materials. Your support of the author's rights is appreciated. Any member of educational institutions wishing to photocopy part or all of the work for classroom use, or anthology, should send inquiries to Grove Atlantic, 154 West 14th Street, New York, NY 10011 or permissions@groveatlantic.com.

Published simultaneously in Canada
Printed in the United States of America

ISBN 978-0-8021-2427-2
eISBN 978-0-8021-9192-2

The Mysterious Press
an imprint of Grove Atlantic
154 West 14th Street
New York, NY 10011

Distributed by Publishers Group West

groveatlantic.com

15 16 17 18   10 9 8 7 6 5 4 3 2 1

For Cara Schlesinger & Otto Penzler

Historical truth, for him, is not what took place; it is what we think took place.
—Jorge Luis Borges, "Pierre Menard, Author of *Don Quixote*"

What object is served by this circle of misery and violence and fear? It must tend to some end, or else our universe is ruled by chance, which is unthinkable. But what end? There is the great standing perennial problem to which human reason is as far from an answer as ever.
—Arthur Conan Doyle, "The Cardboard Box"

THEY NEVER FOUND his hands. For days into weeks they searched the windswept coast south of the Montauk highway, fanning out into the icy scrub that edged the dunes, combing miles of coastline looking for a possible small makeshift grave where the pair might be buried. February flurries and short daylight hours hampered their efforts, erasing any telltale disturbances in the sand and semifrozen dirt. Speculating that the severed hands might possibly wash up on shore if his attacker had thrown them out into the churning surf, they scoured the shallows during low tides. Unless salt water had scrubbed his fingernails clean, there was a chance his nails might harbor forensic evidence—especially if he had fought with his assailant, which the disarray at the crime scene suggested he had. Still, the search turned up nothing. It was as if his hands had simply joined together at the wrists, become a pair of wings, and flown away across the gray Atlantic.

The poor wretch survived ten days in the intensive care unit of a New York hospital where he had been transported at his sister's request. In and mostly out of consciousness, he was unable to speak to either his sibling or the police because whoever dismembered his hands had first struck him with brutal precision on the back of his head—he had been working at his desk quietly, as was his solitary predawn habit—leaving him unconscious in a bath of coagulating blood on the floor of his beachfront studio.

The intruder, it seemed, had been expert at his grisly task or else lucky in the extreme. No signs of forced entry. Marble rolling pin used to crack the victim's skull was from his own kitchen. Neither footprints nor fingerprints found. No valuables had been stolen, no money, no jewelry. A vintage Patek Philippe Calatrava, an heirloom from his father, lay unmolested, its second hand tracing serene circles, on the victim's desk. And because the altercation had occurred sometime before sunrise, neighbors had seen nothing unusual in what dim gray-green light the early winter day afforded. After the savagery, it seemed the intruder, much like the hands, had vaporized. None among the regular ragtag of sunrise joggers, who daily ran up and down the beach no matter what the weather, and sleepy dog walkers bundled against the chill had seen anything suspicious. Nor had anyone nearby been awakened by shouts or screams, the incessant crash and hiss of the ocean's waves having drowned out any such noise, if noise there had been. Besides, all the windows on either side of the house were closed, their curtains drawn tight.

When the postman arrived early on his route to deliver another of the many parcels that came to this address from here and there around the world, he found the front door ajar, which made no sense given how cold the weather was. Over the years, he and the victim had become if not friends then friendly acquaintances, which made it all the more unbearable that, after calling out softly then loudly, over and over, stepping unsure and trembling into the foyer—this was a day he had hoped would never happen to him or anyone else he knew—he discovered the body at the far end of the cottage. Even after an ambulance and police vehicles pulled into the narrow lane in front of the cottage, shattering the peace of this solitary neighborhood like meteors hitting a monastery, the man with no hands was still clinging, with a firm spirit if little else, to life.

The most puzzling discovery investigators made at the scene was of a number of handwritten letters and manuscripts by political and literary lights from earlier eras, all scattered in chaos around the studio. Rare books also carpeted the floor, their covers splayed like dead birds, inscription pages torn from many of the bindings. Lincoln and Twain, Churchill and Dickens, a trove of Arthur Conan Doyle documents lay together with dozens of others. Most had been vandalized, ripped to shreds or spattered with blood and ink from an array of antique ink pots once neatly arranged in a cabinet but now tossed about. Whether any manuscripts or signed books were missing was difficult to determine since there appeared to be no catalogue of the collector's holdings, and a check later with his insurance company would reveal that they hadn't been scheduled or insured. But because so many other valuables had not been taken, including books in cases that lined the walls of the studio, the prevailing assumption was that no literary treasures had been stolen, either. What possible logic would dictate the assailant destroy so much precious holograph material only to steal away with others? No, the felonies here appeared to be wanton destruction of valuable property and a severe assault with probable intent to kill, not mere theft.

When Adam Diehl finally died, anything he might have been able to say about the assault—who was behind it, what motivated such barbarity—perished with him. To this day, it grieves me to acknowledge that his death under the circumstances was a tragic if godsent blessing given what an appalling life, mute and prosthetic, he surely would have faced had he survived. Sign language and even speech, given the brain damage that resulted from his head trauma, would have been forever beyond his grasp. He had been, according to his sister, Meghan, ever a recluse, but his injuries would decidedly have isolated him far beyond whatever pleasures he took from living the phantom life. No, surely it was better to lie peacefully in a pretty, manicured cemetery than suffer through the daily grind of such disablement. Isn't the butterfly whose wings have been plucked by a heedless child better off crushed beneath his heel than left in the grass gazing up at the sky, flightless?

Meghan, whom I'd been seeing for a few years before this incident took place, called me with the horrid news. She was sobbing so hysterically that her breath came in jerky bursts and her words cascaded in raw fragments over the sketchy cell phone connection. Hearing the cries of children at play in the background—why weren't they in school?—I realized she had left work for the comparatively more private precincts of Tompkins Square to reach out to me. Not knowing what to say, I said nothing, but just listened to her, my beloved Meg, as she told me everything she knew about what had happened. I remember feeling numb and dislocated, alone at my kitchen table, wishing for all the world I was right there with her, kissing away her tears, holding her tight against me.

Divorced, sweet-spirited, an unpretentious, even earthy woman with flame-red hair who in her late thirties could easily pass for someone ten years younger, Meghan ran a used-book shop in the East Village that specialized in her twin fields of interest, art and cooking. She had learned early on to be independent when she and Adam were orphaned in their preteens—boating accident off Montauk, where the family owned the small beachfront house that Adam later appropriated for his studio hermitage—and were raised in Manhattan by a bookish aunt. In those childhood years they had grown unusually close, relied on each other for support and companionship, behaved themselves in front of their bibulous guardian but created a childhood world of their own, one that for a number of years was only really populated by two. Though Adam was the elder sibling, Meghan had always been more outgoing, so she sheltered him in a way, even mothered him at times. Generous to a fault, she let him have the Montauk residence and, as I began to notice, had often paid his bills when he fell behind. As she filled me in on what last details she knew about his injuries, I pictured her in the square, walking alone beneath the barren trees in the drizzle under heavy purple clouds, and my heart went out to her.

"Where is he now?" I asked, trying to be calm enough for both of us.

"They've taken him to an emergency room in Southampton."

"So he's alive," I said. "That's promising, right?"

"Just barely, he's critical, they told me he lost a lot of blood—" and she broke down crying again.

I waited a little before asking, "Meg, when did all this happen? Do they know who did it?"

"This, this morning," she answered. I assumed that her ignoring my second question meant she knew they didn't, or maybe it wasn't a priority for her just then.

Since I owned a car—a true city girl, Meghan didn't know how to drive—I offered to take her out to the hospital right away. We would have to rent one, as mine was in the repair shop, but that presented no problem, I assured her.

"God, I don't know if I can face seeing him. Is that bad?"

"Of course not. He probably wouldn't even know if you were there with all the drugs they must have him on," I reassured her. Then, "You want me to come meet you?"

"Later, yes," she said, abruptly having stopped weeping. "It's nice of you to offer, especially since you never really liked my brother."

"I never said that," was all I could manage, and though she wasn't entirely wrong about my feelings, I admit I was dumbstruck it would occur to her to say such a thing under the circumstances. But Meghan was devastated, I reminded myself, overwhelmed by such unexpected, staggering news. It was imperative I say nothing to risk our spiraling into some needless, counterproductive quarrel. My job wasn't to contradict but to let her know she wasn't alone, that she could count on me. She had, after all, been a rock for me at a time when I needed support not long after I first began dating her. Now it was my turn.

"Look," I ventured. "I'm sure he'll be okay. He's a healthy guy, so that's in his favor. People survive worse."

News of Adam Diehl's assault stirred a lot of interest in the rare book world, at least for a time, even though he was not a major player or even a figure who was all that well known in the trade. Everyone was deeply disturbed by the events, horrified that one of their own, a fellow book lover, would suffer such a macabre attack. At the same time, the usual questions everyone outside this rarefied literary community asked—who did this? wasn't Montauk always such a safe place?—were supplemented by a profound interest in the books themselves. Who would wantonly destroy books of such quality? Who knew that this Diehl fellow had amassed such an extensive collection? And what was going to happen to the books that weren't destroyed? No one asked me anything outright, about either the collector or his library, but my relationship with his sister was generally known, and I could sense the unasked questions behind expressions of condolence and concern from fellow bookmen.

After Adam was transported to New York City, I did accompany Meghan to the hospital once before he passed away. Her anguish at seeing him, wrists and head bandaged, leashed to an impressive array of machinery, ignited in me a mosaic of conflicting responses. As anyone would be, I was agonized by Meghan's grief and fear and appalled to see him lying there in such a state, helpless in the carnival-bright, less-than-antiseptic ICU. Despite the detail in which she had already described his injuries, I had not expected his condition would be quite this bad—I pictured him gravely maimed, not in mortal danger. Yet at the same time, I was still smarting from her comment about my uneasy relationship with her brother, which left me in the unenviable position of having to pretend I was more upset by his state than, in shameful reality, I was. I don't care to admit it, but a kind of melancholy emotional paralysis veiled itself behind my expressions of loving concern. No civilized person likes to see a fellow human suffering, and I do believe myself to be, despite any faults I might have, civilized. In short, it was a sorry vigil and I did my level best to measure up.

"Adam," Meghan whispered, breaking the unhappy silence of the room as she leaned close to his gauze-obscured face. Bruises beneath his eyes made him look as if he hadn't slept for a year, while his aquiline nose gave him a kind of dignity amid the ruin. I had never before noticed that his was almost identical to his sister's nose. "Adam, honey. I'm right here pulling for you. Everybody is."

He did not—could not?—respond.

When Meghan side-glanced me, nodding toward her brother, inviting me to add a few words of encouragement, my numbness morphed into a further deepening sadness for her. It seemed inevitable that she was going to be left without any family in this world, the aunt who raised her having died around the time Meghan and I first started dating, and I would soon enough constitute whatever "family" she had.

Taking my cue, I whispered, "Adam, I want to echo what Meghan said, if you can hear us. You've got great care here, the best. You just hang in—"

His eyes, which had been closed, came half-open as his head turned a painful inch toward me on his pillow.

"Adam?" blurted Meghan, hope rising in her voice.

"I'll go get somebody," I told her, and hurriedly left the room.

By the time I returned a minute later, following his day nurse into the room, he had slipped back into a semicoma while Meghan stroked his once-again unresponsive face. As we were leaving the hospital, she did register surprise at his reaction to my presence, saying, a little plaintively, "He seemed to recognize your voice more than mine."

"Like I said before, I don't think he's really capable of recognizing anybody what with all the drugs they have him on. He just seemed to be in a lot of pain suddenly."

"You're probably right."

"Look, main thing is I'm glad we were there to help as best we could."

"Me too," she said, slipping her arm around my waist. "I'm glad you came with me."

"No more of this business about me not liking your brother, okay?"

"I'm sorry I said that. Promise I won't do it again," and drew me closer.

Relieved, even feeling a little vindicated, I leaned over and kissed her before hailing a cab back downtown.

Adam died a few days later. Although Meghan went to visit her brother every morning and evening, I'm embarrassed to admit I came up with legitimate excuses that kept me away from the hospital after that first visit. I made up for my pitiful absence at his bed-side by throwing all of my best energies into helping her arrange for cremation and burial. Close as we had long been, we were never closer than during that time. She spent every night over at my floor-through just off Irving Place, near Gramercy Park. We quietly cooked dinner together, me acting the role of sous-chef as she grilled scallops one evening and roasted duck another. Sleepless, we shared wine and screened old science fic-tion flicks like *Metropolis* and *The Island of Lost Souls*. We made love with a fervor only a close encounter with death can inspire in the living. In the simplest of ways, we embraced life by embracing each other. To be sure, Adam was never too far from our minds throughout this period of survivalist mourning, with Meghan remembering happy moments from their past and me listening to each one, knowing that these memories were her best legacy and, as such, were to be respected.

Each of us had already been separately interviewed by the investigators and, after exhausting and even de-meaning hours of interrogation, deemed not to be, in that wretched phrase, "persons of interest." That they had shown particular interest in me was unnerving, to say the least, but after discovering I was home asleep and had neither motive nor means they let me go and pursued whatever meager leads they had. They brought in others for questioning, as well, a few from the rare book field, all of whom appeared to have passable alibis. Asked if I knew this dealer or that collector, I answered honestly that I did and considered them all to be above reproach, for whatever my opinion was worth.

Meanwhile, the press, initially drawn to the maiming and murder of Adam Diehl, began to lose interest. One hometown tabloid had dubbed the slaying "The Manuscript Murder." Despite the mildly clever alliterative, the phrase didn't gain much traction—who in the tabloid public gives a good goddamn about literary manuscripts, not to mention rare books?—and the story itself faded from the near-front pages toward the middle and then out of rotation sooner than I or anyone else in the book trade, peripheral or otherwise, might have expected.

During this time, Meghan and I cocooned ourselves away from others, which allowed her, whose resilience profoundly impressed me, a chance to begin her process of healing. We did find ourselves inevitably returning to the subject of who might possibly have wanted to hurt Adam, slay him in such a way, with Meghan concluding there was a strong chance it was someone we didn't even know.

"He had his own life out in Montauk," she said, with frustrated resignation. "Close as we were, there's all kinds of things I'm sure he kept from his little sister."

I nodded, thinking, Truer words were never uttered.

DYING IS A DANGEROUS BUSINESS. A liberation from suffering, a release from life's problems, death is also an indictment. Once we're dead, secrets that we so carefully nurtured, like so many black flowers in a veiled garden, are often brought out into the light where they can flourish. Cultivated by truth, fertilized by rumor, they blossom into florets and sprays that are toxic to those who would sniff their poisonous perfumes. While I did my best to shelter Meghan from certain unsavory discoveries that were made about her brother's life—like many a sibling, she understandably didn't want to believe he was anything other than an innocent victim—some damning details would soon enough vine their strangling way into the light. Details that, as fate would have it, I had already surmised about Adam but could not before his death practically or honorably reveal to her. Details that I myself was duty bound to help transit from that darkness of secrecy into truth's awkward glare. Salt on the wound, I know, and yet it would prove to be an unavoidable seasoning.

Now that I am on the subject of truth, it is important that I offer a confession. Or, rather, an illumination in order to bring into better focus Adam Diehl's unfortunate death and by way of explaining how I knew what I knew, or believed I knew, about his hidden life.

You see, like Adam, I myself was once a forger. Undeniably, and even unashamedly, triumphantly a forger. There was a time in my life when nothing gave me more joy than forging letters and manuscripts by my favorite writers. Nor was I some naif off the boat who was taken in and, if you will, pimped out by dealers who used my unique handiwork to make millions for themselves while I was left the breadcrumbs. No, I knew who I was and what I was doing. I learned the ropes and forged, ha, my path. And I adored my job. It is no exaggeration to state that the tremulous thrill that surged through me when I lowered my nib to virgin paper was the most erotic feeling I could possibly imagine, the most intoxicating, the most resplendent. The satisfaction of virtuosity put to the test was like none other, was what I lived for and what Diehl possibly strived for, too, though I suspect the gentle art of forgery never gave him the visceral stab of pleasure that it invariably gave me. When I conceived and penned the inscription of an esteemed master in a copy of his or her rarest book—sometimes to a family member, other times to a fellow novelist or poet—an edgy sublimity settled over the moment. It was like electric stardust, say, or a kind of aurora borealis of the mind. Truly, happiness beyond words.

Part of what lay behind this unique feeling was the high-wire nature of the act itself. As a skilled craftsman, the forger has but one chance to get it just right, or else instead of making a book more desirable, more valuable, he has wrecked the thing. But when it is done expertly—and in my heyday I was nothing if not an expert, I think perhaps the finest expert at work during my transient time in the trade—heaven shone down and a choir of rebel angels sang. The rest was about the tense, satisfying pleasure of knowing something others might only try and fail to guess at. Whenever I sold my handiwork to an experienced bookseller for a considerable sum, I knew I had once again hoodwinked the world even as I had ironically made it a richer, more luminous place. I thought—rightly in the beginning, wrongly later—I could rest assured that my spurious inscribed books, my fake letters and manuscripts could travel the precincts of bibliographic connoisseurship with the perfect invisibility of the authentic, above reproach, for all intents and purposes *real*. Such refined beguilement was the alpha and omega of my art.

For most of my adult life I was a man who was all about ink and paper and first editions. Vintage papers for early correspondence and holograph manuscripts, hand-mixed inks, irreproachable, for lavish inscriptions. Not words so much as letters, their connectors and flow, were what mattered most to me, at least in the beginning, back when I was starting out. Each letter required the right presence and pressure, the tender weight of ink, old sepia, faded black, on my small canvas. The ascenders, the descenders, the choreographic shape and spirit of a comma, these were what kept me up at night. The precision of a period. Single quotes like

black crescent moons in a parchment sky. The adage
has it, *Do what you love*. This was what I loved.

Then I got caught. The industry—a small subcul-
ture where pebbles dropped in a pond can create tidal
waves; a tribe of brilliant children—roiled for a while in
the aftermath of my conviction. Perhaps "roiled" is too
strong a word, a little egotistical of me to frame it in such
a way. Still, as I was later told by a number of friends in
the trade who, despite my downfall, would eventually remain friends, various perfectly authentic letters and signatures in all manner of first editions were suddenly suspect,
and some dealers were as loath to buy as collectors. The
same experts who before had bought my offerings with
utmost confidence were now questioned by special collections librarians and others who wanted reappraisals
of authenticity for works acquired during my admitted
years of activity, especially when it came to authors that
had been my specialty, Conan Doyle and Sherlockiana
being at the top of that list. Parts of the autograph market
briefly stalled, as markets do when doubt is injected into
their body politic, but not for long, especially given what a
comparatively small niche I had occupied.

Whether it was because I was represented by a
shrewd attorney, which I was, and a wise and respectable man to boot, or because this particular lily-white
collar crime was one that the police and prosecutors
didn't take as seriously as other scams—it was far more
sexy to bust an insider trading hedge fund bigwig than
some fellow who could write an H. G. Wells postcard—
I managed to get a good plea bargain. I had never been
in trouble with the law before, didn't have so much as
a parking ticket in my record, and that naturally helped
me, too. The fact that I hadn't stolen anything, as such,

further figured into my overall picture as a positive factor. After consulting with my lawyer, I confessed—no need for the bother of a trial—and was convicted and sentenced.

In exchange for my full cooperation and in light of that prior clean record, punishment was limited to probation, a substantial fine, repayment plus interest to buyers, what seemed like endless hours of community service sweeping leaves and litter in city parks, and an agreement going forward to help the authorities identify forgeries like the ones I used to make with such aplomb. The pact I made with myself was that I would turn a new leaf. Many bridges had been burned, I knew, but rare book dealers, lest I depict them wrongly as a community of authorities that could be duped, are for the most part very sharp, honest, and thoughtful individuals. When asked by the police if I felt forgery was rampant in the trade, I told them no, that, with all modesty, it took someone of my caliber and sophistication to get past any of them. Lesser practitioners were inevitably shot out of the sky like low-flying birds. Not to brag, but it took a raptor like myself to clear the range of their canny buckshot, at least while my long flight lasted. Over time, to my great relief and even joy, a number of people forgave or forgot—I was always well liked in the industry and I insisted wherever and as often as I could that most of the books and manuscripts I handled were not forged, a courteous lie that no one could disprove—my reputation was slowly rehabilitated. I even did freelance work at one of the auction houses, vetting upcoming lots for possible impostors among the literary jewels that collectively brought millions in their rooms.

So, yes, my dirty secret was exposed, my cherished *affaire de coeur* with pen and paper was over. I suffered as a result—and deservedly—but also strove for and mostly attained my redemption, though of course there were some people in the trade who shunned me forever after.

The posthumous revelations of Diehl's secrets, on the other hand, so to say, left the man unshielded, and because of the tenuous dots that connected him and me via Meghan, I wasn't overly surprised that the investigators called me back in. When they explained they wanted me, of all people, to have a look at some of the damaged books and manuscripts, I figured the exercise had as much to do with giving me yet another look as a possible suspect as it did with confirming or denying the items were forgeries or materials were forger's tools. I showed up on time—confident but not overly confident, friendly but not suspiciously friendly—with the simple desire to give them the information they sought and be back home in New York that night in time for dinner with Meghan as usual.

Did I recognize any of these items? they asked, handing me a tray and then others with dried blood- and ink-soaked documents in them opened to pertinently inscribed pages or leaves. Grateful I didn't have to wear surgical gloves because I wasn't asked to touch anything, I honestly answered, No. That is, for instance, I recognized that this was the first edition of Dickens's *American Notes* published in London in 1842, both volumes sadly torn out of their bindings but with a contemporary inscription and Dickens's characteristic Slinky of narrower and narrower squiggles beneath his signature looking plausibly correct. But did I recognize this specific volume? No.

What would something like that be worth? they asked.

In fine condition, as it might have been before the incident, and if the recipient here was a friend of the author—I couldn't make out the name, I apologized—perhaps fifty to seventy-five.

Dollars?

Yes, well, thousand dollars I mean.

I was puzzled when they asked me if I had ever heard of one Henry Slader, to whom Adam had been apparently paying monthly installments for some acquisition or another. Regarding him, I could only shrug. "Nothing unusual about installments," I told them. Not being used to the high prices rare books often traded for, they expressed particular interest in the fact that thousands of dollars were in play here.

"Nothing unusual about the money, either," I assured them. "Like that Dickens we were just looking at, these aren't your everyday run-of-the-mill books we're talking about."

Their turn to shrug.

The interrogation or consultation, whatever it was, went along like this for an hour or more before they arrived at some questions I had more or less anticipated, given they could get others to do their verifications and appraisals for them.

Just a few more things that interested them, if I didn't mind. Did Adam Diehl and I ever discuss forgery? Did we ever do business together? Did he ever approach me, as his sister's boyfriend, for any favors or advice regarding forgeries?

No, no, and no, I told them, forthright and if anything a little insulted. Maybe my mild annoyance showed or maybe it didn't. Either way, I answered all their questions to the best of my knowledge. Had they a lie detector and examiner there, I would gladly have agreed to answer again and let the inky needle's failure to jump reassure them.

What I could say, and did, was that some of the regrettably damaged works were not fakes, as far as I could tell, and that they could run my opinions regarding each individual item past any number of other specialists in literary artifacts and they would find most if not all of them would likely concur with me. They assured me they would do just that, thanked me, and said I could go. I sensed they might have been disappointed, but what did I know?

While I had over the years strongly suspected him of being a member of my erstwhile fraternity of forgers, I had never brought the matter up with Diehl, just as I told the cops, and obviously I never betrayed any of my suspicions to Meghan. But when, over a glass of wine before dinner, I revealed where I had been that day and the sorts of questions the authorities were asking me about forgery, rather than being concerned how it went, she rebuked me for not having told her I was called in, first, and second, that I had any idea about Adam and forgery.

I said, "I know I should have told you they called, but I guess I wanted to protect you from having to worry about it. You've got enough on your hands as it is. And as for Adam, you're all too aware I didn't know him that well. Did I ever even lay eyes on his collection?"

No need to relate every turn of the screw as our evening spiraled downward from there. Suffice it to say the poor woman turned on me for a few really rotten days and nights, threatened never to see me again. She was,

and I state this with a curious sort of admiration, harder
on me than the police had been.

"How could you not have known about Adam?
There's no way you couldn't have known," she said, her
voice tight, her face half as red as her hair.

"Suspecting and knowing are two very different animals," I countered.

"Do you understand how humiliating this is? What
if it gets around everywhere?" she asked. "My customers
will laugh behind my back, or worse, they'll feel sorry
for me. I could lose my business."

"But you, you haven't done anything wrong. Nobody's accusing you of anything. And nobody but you
is accusing me of anything, either."

"Between you and now Adam, why should anybody
trust me any more? Why should I even trust myself?"

Knowing I might better keep my mouth shut, but
in a fit of exasperation, I said, "Speaking of trust. When
they questioned you, did you tell them you thought I
didn't like your brother? Is that why they dragged me
back in today?"

"I never said anything of the kind."

"Because I couldn't help but wonder, while I was
sitting in their airless room going around in circles with
them, if that wasn't why I was there."

It went on like that, my feeble attempt at accusation
having fallen flat. She suspected me of having been a
pernicious influence on Adam, even of having worked
secretly with him, all kinds of crazy things. I'd never
seen her act like this before and was at a loss what to do
beyond telling her she was wrong.

Eventually the hostility, or anger, or shame, or the
thorny combination of all of those and more passed.

Meghan and I had weathered tough times in the past and we were going to get through this one, too. What she didn't know, could never know, was that even if I had bothered to work with her brother, my influence on him would have been beneficial rather than pernicious—at least to his craft—but that I would never in a hundred millennia have shared my techniques, my supply sources, my tools, my *passion* with Adam Diehl or anybody else. It is possible that although she couldn't fathom why I so adamantly denied having anything to do with Adam's forgery, the adamancy itself and the indisputable truth of my denial finally got through to her.

When we made up, strolling through Tompkins Square for coffee while she was on a lunch break, I told her, "Look, Meg, after what you've been through, it's a wonder you've held yourself together as well as you have."

A cynic might see these words as clichéd, but they were offered in good faith. And sometimes, in the right circumstances, even the simplest cliché can carry profound weight. If, as Emerson wrote, every word was once an idea, every cliché was once a revelation.

DESPITE MY EFFORTS TO THE CONTRARY and even as Meghan and I grew closer after our brief argument, Adam haunted my thoughts. Whether I was helping her in the bookshop or doing authentication and cataloguing at the auction house where I'd settled into as close to a permanent position as I ever would have, he was a ghostly presence. I would always be grateful for his bringing along his sister, some half-dozen years back, to the book fair where I first met her—a gratitude I never bothered expressing because I knew without asking how our early flirtations and eventual relationship chafed at him—but there wasn't much else about the fellow that drew anything from me akin to warm amicability.

I don't remember for sure the first time I laid eyes on him, though I recognized the man in a nebulous across-the-room sort of way some years before I even knew he had a sister and well before my forger's days came to a dismal end. Adam Diehl was one of those people who slowly dawned on you. Who you realize, without giving it conscious thought, is someone you have seen before but didn't know. His maker had given him a nondescript face, which probably aided him in his line of work. To say his skin was sallow might be a little mean-spirited, but that he could live beside the sea and maintain such a candle-wax complexion spoke volumes as to how little time he spent outdoors. He was thinner and taller than most, loose-jointed, one might say even willowy. He shared with Meghan, as I'd later find out when he introduced us, a head of wavy red hair and eyes the color of Noodler's Baystate blue ink, emblems of their Irish heritage—indeed, Meghan had been born in the land of Yeats, Joyce, and Beckett, and had dual citizenship though she hadn't visited the old country since childhood. His dress was studiously decades out of style, an eccentricity I admit I found kind of endearing. His inveterate blue-black blazer with its gold-trimmed crest-of-arms pocket patch, his white shirt and narrow black tie, even his gabardine trousers hung on his frame as if upon a secondhand-shop mannequin. Not unhandsome, he stood out from the crowd largely because of his height, hair, and tortoiseshell bifocals. Also, he had the thinnest wrists I had ever seen on a man and the most elegant, tapered fingers.

Overall, an eccentric, an odd duck. But then antiquarian book fairs are, to mix a metaphor, beehives of odd ducks, and this dawning of Diehl occurred at rare book shows over the years, such as the annual international gathering of dealers at the Armory on Park

Avenue. Once his presence did take hold, I noticed that he and I frequented many of the same specialists' booths.

There is a bookseller out there for every bibliophilic obsession known to humankind. You want a seventeenth-century book on microscopy with engraved illustrations on the life cycle of mosquitoes? There is a dealer who can provide you with that. You fancy rare volumes on Antarctic exploration or the history of ancient Egyptians? Not a problem. Perhaps a first edition, first printing of Jonathan Swift's *Travels into Several Remote Nations of the World, by Lemuel Gulliver* or the 1813 triple-decker of Jane Austen's *Pride and Prejudice* in contemporary calf? These can be had. With money, patience, and an obsessive hawk eye, there are few books in the world that cannot be taken home to place on a shelf or in a safe. Librarians and collectors, from high rollers to those of more modest means, converged with calendric regularity at the big Armory show and other such fairs around the world. And many of these bibliophiles became business acquaintances if not friends over time.

Slowly, vaguely, I began to notice that Diehl and I were mostly interested in the same literary autograph materials, such as inscribed books and original holograph manuscripts from the nineteenth and twentieth centuries. I would like to think I wasn't stalking him, but after walking into this or that bookseller's booth and hearing more than once that another gentleman had just shown interest in the same item, studying it with great care, I found it impossible not to take heed. Who was this guy with shared tastes and a penchant for admiring at length the penmanship of Churchill and Conan Doyle?

"You mind my asking what else he looked at?" was a question I found myself posing with increased frequency and not a little hesitation. Some sellers, the more seasoned ones, shrugged off my cheeky question with slight not-unfriendly smiles that read, You know I can't do that. But others, whether from carelessness or simply an eagerness to flaunt their wares, showed me this Thomas Hardy letter or that Wilkie Collins inscription that Diehl had held in his hands not long before. The more I learned about his tastes, the more I was intrigued by him even as a small wary voice in my head advised me to be careful.

Now and again I did buy a manuscript, a letter, an inscribed first edition. Not only didn't I want to be perceived as a stiff—even the most lackadaisical merchant is there to sell, not simply show—but I liked to take home some of the best examples I found by my favorite authors in order to analyze their every nuance under a gooseneck magnifying glass in the solitude of my study. I knew I could always auction them off later or make a private sale, at cost or even a modest loss, and still come out ahead of the game thanks to knowledge gained. Unless run to ground, forgers always come out ahead. Nature of the beast. Although, as in any vocation, those who truly love their work would embrace it with every fiber of their being even if there were nothing but a plug nickel at the rainbow's end. For me, the pot of gold was in the act itself, even if the act produced but fool's gold.

On a Saturday afternoon in April some half-dozen years ago, standing elbow to elbow in the booth of a gregarious London dealer with leonine unkempt hair and disheveled tweed suit, Diehl and I were finally introduced. I had just handed back an inscribed first edition

of Darwin's *On the Origin of Species*, having spent a
good deal of time studying the inscription, its date and
place, its recipient, and above all the calligraphy and
signature, when Diehl materialized like an apparition
at my side, softly coughed, and asked the dealer if he
might have a look at it too before it went back into the
glass display case between Freud's *Die Traumdeutung*
and a signed copy of Ludwig Wittgenstein's *Tractatus*,
each in astonishingly fine condition.

"I'm sure you two must know each other?" said the
genial dealer.

Diehl and I turned and looked at one another.

"I don't, I'm afraid," he said, although I sensed his
eyes betrayed a subtle recognition of me. The unmodu-
lated tone of his voice, flat as a folio's flyleaf, was un-
readable. I had always been far better at interpreting
inanimate manuscripts than living voices and the looks
on people's faces.

"Don't think so," I said, not quite lying but not exactly telling the truth—a tit-for-tat.

We shook hands and I offered a platitude about
the Darwin, something about how it amazed me that
such a rare book could at the same time be so common.
There were at least several available at the fair.

"Money is always a nice incentive," the dealer said,
joining in with his own platitude.

"Too rich for my blood," offered Diehl, as he handed
the volume back and, after saying it was nice to meet
me, left.

"Collector?" I enquired, feigning naivete, having
noticed that this Diehl fellow was rarely if ever to be
seen carrying purchases, mummified in clear plastic bags,
under his arm.

"More a scout. He's sold me some good things over the years, though he surprises me now and again by buying the occasional gem. Not unlike yourself."

"Oh," I said, and turned my head to glance at him as he disappeared down the aisle crowded with fairgoers.

Of course, neither Diehl nor I were ever, strictly speaking, scouts, other than to scout out nice copies of unsigned firsts that could after a "cooling period" re-enter the market duly autographed or fulsomely inscribed by their respective authors—or else pick up inexpensive, relatively unimportant period books and manuscripts with blank leaves that, extracted, could become canvases for newly created period manuscripts or letters. After that initial encounter, I began to suspect who and what he really was and, as discreetly as I could manage, asked those in my closest coterie of dealers where they happened to acquire this inscribed volume or that autograph letter. It seemed to me that more Conan Doyle documents were surfacing than usual, and because Sherlock Holmes had always been my favorite, my meat and potatoes, my black clay pipe and deerstalker hat if you will, I was keenly attuned to such minutiae. Fair or not, logical or not, I became convinced that Diehl was the primary source for this rising tide of inscribed and holograph Holmes materials. As I started looking into the matter I recalled the sleuth's housekeeper, Mrs. Hudson, in the Sherlock Holmes movie *The Spider Woman*, who at one point proclaims, "What can't be cured must be endured." For better or worse, I have seen all the celluloid Sherlocks, from Basil Rathbone to Jeremy Brett, and while I far prefer Sir Arthur Conan Doyle's tales to anything caught on film, that line stuck to me like a newly noticed birthmark.

And much as I might hate a birthmark, I hated this
sentiment. Not only are there myriad ways to avoid enduring the incurable but, other than a malignant tumor
or some other terminal illness, I believe there is nothing
that cannot be cured. You see, I am fundamentally an
optimist.

I began by questioning the authenticity of what
were, to my honed eye, possible fakes. In my own work,
any time I made even the most insignificant mistake
when forging an inscription, I bit the bullet and either
discarded the volume in disgust or single-edge-razored
out the flawed leaf and then sold the amputated book
to a secondhand shop for a fraction of the money I had
originally paid. I never allowed anything out of my win-
dowless, well-lit workshop that wasn't first-tier quality.
Others were less scrupulous. So whenever I discovered
a small anomaly, I respectfully and privately brought
it to the attention of whatever dealer had it in stock.
I was cautious not to make a nuisance of myself and
didn't bother alerting anyone to signatures that were
conspicuously bogus—let somebody else point out that
William Burroughs, not my era but just for instance,
rarely dotted the "i"s in his first name—but near misses,
professional work with a telltale Achilles' heel, were
fair game.

Just before Memorial Day that same spring, knowing of my lifelong interest in all things Sherlockian, my
favorite bookseller, Atticus Moore, up in Providence,
gave me a ring and told me he had acquired a large
group of remarkable letters written by Conan Doyle
in May and June 1901 to Greenhough Smith, editor of
the *Strand Magazine*. Seventeen letters in all, they detailed at length progress being made on the manuscript

of what would become *The Hound of the Baskervilles*, which the *Strand* published later that same year. Though they appeared never to have been mailed for some reason and were apparently unpublished, all the biographical points checked out, according to my friend. Written from Devon, they described in fresh detail precisely how Doyle had gotten the original idea from a journalist acquaintance, Bertram Fletcher Robinson, while vacationing at the Royal Links Hotel on a headland overlooking the North Sea in Norfolk. A draft passage set in Grimpen Mire, based on the real-life bog, Fox Tor Mire, that never made it into the published manuscript was penned on the verso of one letter and then crossed out. In another letter, Conan Doyle describes having privately witnessed a midnight apparition out his mullioned window after having visited Park Hall, the ancient Robinson manor house on which Baskerville Hall probably was based, an apparition he dared not mention to his companions as it too closely resembled the monstrous, mythological hound of his story-in-progress—a monster "best confined to the precincts of memory." The letter concluded he would retain "an inquisitorial attitude" about the vision, although he fails to mention it further in the subsequent epistles.

It was as unique and historically interesting a clutch of letters as my dealer friend had ever handled. Given the letters were written by my favorite writer from childhood to this day, a writer of exquisite, enviable cunning and a craftsman of the first order, I knew immediately that they had to be mine no matter the cost. He asked if I would like to run up to Providence to see them and have a late lunch afterward.

I would and did, grabbing the first train north the very next morning. As I watched the inlets along the Connecticut coast pass by, the sailing boats and osprey nests on their stilts, my mind itself traveled in different directions. Part of me urgently hoped this unposted correspondence was genuine, as I would dearly love to add it to my small "permanent" collection—I incarcerate the word *permanent* within quotes because I think it is one of the most fraudulent words in the English language, and signifies an incontestable falsehood. Another part, however, suspected the letters and that unpublished manuscript fragment were simply too good to be true—much like the idea of permanence—even though my friend was one of the most respected authorities in the world.

After looking them over for an hour and haggling out a fair purchase price, by which I mean hefty but not eviscerating, we had an excellent downtown meal at Capriccio, his treat, and I was back in New York that same evening with my newly acquired trove. To say I was excited would be misleading in that these essentially worthless pieces of paper for which I had paid a good deal of not-worthless money were not destined for the permanent collection. No, the whole lot was a fraud. But it was far and away the finest forgery I had seen in many a year, perhaps ever, inventive in its content, convincing in its execution. I was awestruck and disturbed and compelled to take it off the market lest it come under wider scrutiny.

A forgery of this high quality is, to my mind, as informed by genius as any of your everyday authentic originals. It's just that the creativity involved is of an altogether different variety. A page upon which the creator of Sherlock Holmes has written a passage, one in which let's say a diabolical murder has taken place, one that's stumped Scotland Yard, one that requires Holmes's powers of deduction to solve, is at the end of the day a literary artifact, nothing more or less. Its significance has everything to do with language, narrative, and imagination, and nothing to do with the author's penmanship. We do not worship gods because they dress well. Many writers from Shakespeare on down have had truly atrocious handwriting. A manuscript by W. B. Yeats is not prized because of his hideous, rushed cursive but instead for the poet's inspired music, his imagery, his vision.

On the other hand, forgery is a visual art form that usually has little to do with such niceties as music, imagery, vision. It has to do with the nuance of calligraphic art, a refined sense of historical materials, the science of empathy. Had I the right rag paper, and minerals to mix a passable Elizabethan ink, I could reproduce a couple of lines of Shakespeare's griffonage from, say, *Titus Andronicus*—

> *Give sentence on this execrable wretch,*
> *That hath been breeder of these dire events. . . .*

—that would, under the right circumstances, separate a foolish collector from his wallet. If one has years of experience, knows what he or she is doing, it isn't all that difficult. The Bard provides the words, the forger his reborn hand. Not, mind you, that I have ever done anything so harebrained as try to pawn off a Shakespeare manuscript. One wants to make money from one's enterprise, not to make the news. Any of the greatest literary forgers in history's hall of fame, forgers so great that collectors today buy their works *as forgeries* for considerable sums—from Thomas Chatterton to William Ireland, George Gordon Byron to Thomas J. Wise—would agree, were they alive and willing to speak the truth.

All of which is simply to underscore why this cache of documents impressed me so. Here was someone audacious enough to invoke both head and hand, not to mention heart. The more I studied the pages, the more my admiration grew. But although I might have loved to meet the progenitor of this surefooted bit of magic, my resolve to outdo what I encountered here bested any impulse to congratulate him on his handiwork. That didn't stop me, however, from making very discreet enquiries of my friend Atticus—yes, his parents were shameless Harper Lee devotees and he always stocked a copy or two of *To Kill a Mockingbird*—as to where he tracked down this luscious trove.

He demurred, as well he might. Dealers who want to stay in business can't go around divulging sources to their buyers, especially a buyer such as myself, one who was deemed by Atticus also to be such a good, productive source. Even, from time to time in the past, a veritable cornucopia. I tucked my question away for a rainy day, one on which he might let down his guard. Nor did I bother him with bald questions about provenance or chain of ownership. Surprisingly few books and manuscripts came with documents of provenance, unlike, say, the art world. Despite my own unusual, dark operation and those of a small handful of others, this was truly a gentlemen's trade, one in which considerable scholarly knowledge and pure commerce made a perfect yin-yang fit.

My next chance came over another meal, this time dinner near our hotel, the Fairmont, in San Francisco, where we were both attending an international book fair. We had each done very well that day—I was at the top of my game about then, with upwards of three dozen writers I could forge with unquestionable mastery—and he was particularly happy about some materials I had sold him before the show.

"It's obscene how you continually find such stunning stuff," he gushed, referring to a small clutch of Jack London letters about his story "When God Laughs"— outside my preferred area of expertise but perfect for his Bay Area clients at the show, one of whom snapped them up for double what Atticus paid me. "Really," he continued. "You should have been a dealer yourself."

"That's what they always told my father," I replied.

"Yes, but your dad was a thoroughbred collector. Everything I ever heard about him was that he always bought and never sold. Even when he upgraded a copy he kept the duplicate."

It never failed to make me uneasy when my father— whose memory was still beloved in the trade even by those who never met him—came up. As a collector, he was among the best in his generation. I could only imagine how ashamed he would have been to see his son rightly accused of being a forger, one whose very first attempts at the craft were made while I was still a youth living under his roof, eating his food, studying his library. Though I often missed him, more often I was grateful he had gone the way of all mortals, failing to live long enough to witness the infamy of his own flesh and blood.

After shaking off this flash of disquiet, I set my fork down and said, "Anyway, I don't have the stomach for it. All the rivalry? The competition over customers? The chase after inventory and running down unpaid receivables? I'm better off staying an amateur here on the sidelines, watching you big boys duke it out."

He thought for a moment. "Don't be silly. You'd be so good at it."

"I'm not being silly, just sane. Besides, I think I'd be terrible. I'm too lazy to work my caboose off like you do, day in and out, not to mention too asocial. Other than buying books and such, I live within my means and that's good enough for me."

"You, lazy? I don't think so. Anyway, if you ever change your mind, I'd take you on as a partner in a heartbeat. You just give the word."

It was flattering, I must admit. Over the years, I had toyed with the idea of going legit—well, not *legit* legit, but going into the business, able to accentuate my stock with a bit of Pygmalion ingenuity, if I so desired—but a wise and cautious voice inside told me I was already plenty public doing what I did. Hanging out a shingle with my name on it only invited scrutiny and therefore trouble. The less known about me, the better.

What my friend didn't know, for instance, was that earlier in the day I had covertly sold to various dealers, each sworn to secrecy and motivated to do so by the promise of future materials, more choice autograph items than any of them could imagine. Bragging rights, to be sure. But bragging wasn't on my menu of possibilities.

"By the way, as your unofficial partner, I'd still like to know where you got all that wonderful Baskerville stuff a while ago."

"That again. God, you do persist. All right," he said, taking another drink of his Pinot. "You've actually met the man, tall with red hair and the tortoiseshell glasses?" I nodded. "But don't you dare let on I told you, and if you approach him directly for materials we'll be partners no more, just so you stand warned."

I promised him I wouldn't, and after dinner picked up the check. We had nightcaps at the hotel bar, mine a double cognac. When he excused himself to head for bed, I indulged in a solo second round, as I figured it wasn't going to be a good night's sleep anyway now that I believed I knew for certain Diehl's secret. Wheeler Diehler, I inwardly smirked, but this bit of sarcasm didn't improve my spirits. If Adam Diehl was a fellow forger with tastes similar to mine, with imaginative projects but imperfect skills, he would, if dealers began doubting his wares and rejecting them as the fakes they were, bring a cumulus of suspicion on others' work, *mine* to be precise.

IT WOULD BE LIKE CALLING a gray sky sunny to suggest that Meghan's life and mine settled into a routine of contentment that spring after Adam's burial, despite the fact we had never been closer. Instead, our daily lives resembled the ups and downs of a serrated saw blade. No one we knew begrudged us our striving toward normalcy, but neither did we try to pretend the murder hadn't happened. The investigation inched forward, we were told, but no suspect had as yet been identified. Frustrated, Meghan cried every day and suffered almost nightly from bad dreams. And as for me, it was all I could do to be there to console and comfort her, and not lose my own ever-tentative balance. Even when not spoken of, Adam was a presence in his very absence.

His small service, held on a blustery March morning under eel-colored clouds that promised sleet, was attended by a dozen people. Most were Meghan's friends, as well as a few kids who worked for her at the bookshop and had caught a predawn bus from the city to offer their support. That only a couple of rare book folks showed up, neither of whom I knew very well, was testimony to what a hermit he had been. I recognized one of the detectives huddled in a dark blue parka with the rest of us, and spotted another guy I didn't know but assumed was a plainclothes cop or investigator there to scope out the mourners, see if anyone unusual turned up. They say the guilty are oftentimes drawn to the scene after committing a crime, curious perhaps to connect psychologically with their misdeed, or their victim, or maybe even themselves, to make something abstract feel tangible. Adam's burial might well be a draw given that the crime scene was not even a dozen miles away at the Diehl bungalow, which sat shuttered until the investigation was wrapped up and Meghan saw her way clear to opening it again. If the authorities hoped to spot their perp lingering among us mourners, their hope seemed to be in vain, telling by the looks on their faces.

The hired minister repeated what Meghan had told him about Adam's interests and achievements, read a little scripture, sang a cappella with a few mourners joining him on that old warhorse hymn "Amazing Grace." Meghan clutched the metal funerary urn against her heavy double-breasted overcoat, and wept a little before handing it to the funeral director who would see to its interment, and that was it. We invited the detective to join us at the modest memorial lunch in a local seafood place—the other fellow had disappeared—but he declined. All the while, a lone photographer absurdly

snapped some shots of the gathering from a diplomatic
distance, hoping perhaps to peddle the images to any
tabloids still interested in the story. I would venture to
guess his mission was about as futile as the detective's.

At lunch, after a few glasses of wine, while others
sang his praises and lamented his untimely death, I
found my mind adrift. If Diehl's murder remained an
open case, a nasty bit of business from my own past,
though nothing as terminal as homicide, remained similarly unresolved. It was nothing I ever liked to dwell on,
and when it did surface in my thoughts, like a swarm of
riled hornets or ancient Greek furies, I usually swatted
it away. Today, however, I couldn't. Why the memory
came to me just then was because I always had my suspicions of who was behind what happened but chose
not to pursue the matter out of respect for Meghan.
Let me explain.

In the mail one day—this would have been half a
decade or so before that gloomy memorial luncheon—I
received a letter, with no return address, that in retrospect would be the harbinger of my undoing.

You shall be revealed, it read. *Your deceptions will
prove you to be nothing more than a common criminal &
not the clever sophisticate you believe yourself to be. Darkness shall one day be upon you.*

I don't scare easily. I wasn't afraid of the dark. I
thrived in the dark. Nor have I ever been so deluded as
to consider myself a clever sophisticate, more a hard-
working laborer and devoted artisan than anything
else. Part of me wanted to laugh off the whole matter and simply go on with my day without further ado.
But what troubled me about this brief note, beside the
fact it was penned in Henry James's distinctive flowing

hand on what appeared to be authentic Lamb House
stationery with its handsome red raised type, was that
I had never shared my secret vocation with anyone.
Not one lover, not one friend, not one confidant. Not
even when I had produced a masterwork that I longed
to boast about did I ever betray myself, my secret self.
A high thick wall stood between my one true vice, as
the world would have seen it, and whatever other misdeeds, transgressions, puny immoralities I might have
blurted to anyone, friend, foe, or indifferent.

So it distressed me that whoever penned this letter—
not in the strictest sense a forgery since it wasn't meant
to dupe me into believing it was actually scribed by
James himself—knew what I was about and threatened
to turn my life upside down. I was not going to allow
that to happen. What was more, as I sat and studied
the document with a magnifying glass, its subtle flaws
began to surface out of the murk of concern it pro-
voked, like an ugly tentacled fish rising to the surface
of some brown, stagnant pond. Whoever managed this
was quite good, in many ways even great—I admired
the James signature, which would pass muster with the
pickiest of autograph experts, not to mention the facsimile letterhead that was a dead ringer for an original.
But there were upwards of half a dozen small graphic
mistakes aside from the fact the author of this nasty
little note made no attempt whatsoever to reproduce
James's magisterial voice. The arcade formations of the
lowercase "m" looked like nearby molehills rather than
the jagged distant mountain peaks of Henry James's
characteristic ems. Word spacing was, I felt, somewhat
tighter than it should be, and the amount of ink flowing
from nib to paper was far too consistent. Such flaws in

craft meant flaws in character, to my mind. It suggested, wrongly as it would turn out, that my invisible defamer might not be quite as terrifying a threat as he portrayed himself.

Be this as it may, after the first flush of shock wore off, my feelings graduated to something I wasn't at all used to. I became angry. Very angry. And anger is not a sensation I like. The letter was postmarked in New York, with the same ZIP code as my apartment, another upsetting taunt. In the absence of a return address where I might respond, there was little—no, there was exactly nothing I could do. To make matters worse, this was only the first in a series of inexplicable and maddening letters that I would receive over the course of the next months. I could not afford to report them to the police or anyone else, for the obvious reason that if I did, my beautiful house of counterfeit cards threatened to come crashing down, and the vocation that gave me such joy might be destroyed forever.

Was it coincidental the letters began arriving not so very long after Meghan and I got serious about our relationship, declared ourselves a couple? Maybe so, maybe not, but if I suspected Adam, the way he acted toward me—polite if awkward, restrained yet sometimes willing to share anecdotes about rare book acquisitions or the gossip that circulates through the arteries and veins of the antiquarian trade like lifeblood—gave me pause, a pause I wished into being for Meghan's sake.

Instinctually, I knew Adam regretted our introduction at the Armory show when she tagged along with him and we were crowded together in a booth, making it hard for him not to offer the gesture without appearing thoroughly rude. She and I spoke with easy camaraderie from our first warm handshake. Seeing as Meghan lived downtown, not all that far from me, we decided to go out for a drink, talk books. She showed interest in my collection, and I wanted to visit her shop. Ours was an instant attraction. Love at first sight, if such a thing existed. Despite the unvarnished chill that emanated from her wary brother in even those initial minutes of my acquaintance with his sister—he stood there like the proverbial third wheel, a flat tire of a man—Meghan and I felt we had known each other our entire lives, an impression we confessed on that first drink date several days later. As we grew closer over the weeks and months, Adam and I, never close, withdrew into a polite remoteness. Sure, I recognized that I cut into the time his sister might otherwise have spent with him, in person or on the phone—he seemed far more needy and attached than she, to such an extent that I began to find it pathological—but what could I do? For my part, I think I tried to reach out, at least enough for appearance's sake. But the one time we set up a date to finally have lunch together—I agreed to do this for Meghan's sake, and given I never once traveled out to the tip of Long Island to visit his place, a Manhattan lunch was the least I could do—he himself canceled at the last minute because of some plumbing emergency that had come up in Montauk. He had to get straight out there to attend to it, some Niagara of a dripping faucet, and we never rescheduled.

As for these noxious letters, though, I had to question what possible motive he would have to threaten his sister's beau, his sister whom he clearly adored and whose happiness was paramount to him. Even if he and I were never warm toward one another, would he have been incensed enough to give in to such impulses?

Looking back, I should probably have saved them, these missives. But what good would it have done? They served to incriminate only me, not the sender. If I hadn't been guilty of pretty much every last thing they accused me of doing, I might have had some recourse. But stew as I might in my personal toxic juices of rage and dread, there was no clear response, so I systematically tore them up and threw them away, flushing them in bits and pieces down the toilet. A frustrating business, as vintage bond, unlike toilet paper, prefers to remain afloat rather than sink. Much like guilt itself, I suppose.

In the midst of this concern, I focused on Meghan and my then-current Conan Doyle projects, including nice inscriptions I'd made in a cache of early books bought in England years ago that were ready to re-engage the world with fresh histories. These afforded me the happiness necessary to get through days spent both figuratively and literally looking over my shoulder. Meg and I loved going out to inexpensive restaurants she'd read about, testing various cuisines, sampling the vast variety of foodie culture that only New York and its boroughs can offer—Russian in Brighton Beach, Jamaican in Canarsie, Polish in Greenpoint, Bengali in Kensington. She ran her bookshop by day, which gave me plenty of time to go about my own literary labors in a basement room I rented pseudonymously, not far from my apartment, paying the landlord in cash every month with a dull regularity meant never to raise an eyebrow.

For all my vague suspicions about Diehl during the couple of years I knew him before those ominous letters began arriving, it wasn't until Meghan invited us both over to celebrate her thirty-fifth birthday that an awkward truth surfaced. As it happens, Yeats was Meghan's favorite poet, and though she'd been born in Ireland she had never visited it as an adult. Her lifetime dream was to see Yeats's grave in Drumcliff one day, row out to the lake isle of Innisfree, climb up to the foot of Ben Bulben, sample beer-battered codfish and chips with a pint of Guinness in Sligo. While I couldn't quite pull off giving her that for her birthday, I did get in touch with a Dublin dealer to purchase a signed limited edition of *A Vision*, privately printed by T. Werner Laurie in 1925. I thought it would make a perfect placeholder of sorts until a trip to Ireland was more feasible. Following a homey dinner of turkey and trimmings, leftovers from Thanksgiving, I handed my girlfriend a flute of champagne I'd just uncorked and gave her my gift.

"Oh, I love this," she exclaimed with an excited hug and kiss, after sipping the bubbly and opening the package. "It's my favorite prose book by Yeats, although I can't claim to completely understand it. His gyres always made me dizzy, but now I'll have to give them another go."

When her brother muttered something about great minds thinking alike as he offered her his present, we all knew what it was. Not *A Vision*, his birthday present was a pretty copy in dust jacket of an early trade edition of the *Collected Poems*, autographed by the poet on the title page.

"Now all you're missing are the plays," he said.

"Don't forget the autobiography, the letters, and essays. Yeats contains multitudes," was her beaming response. "This is amazing. You guys must have worked it out together."

We assured her that we were as surprised as she.

"Well, what a wonderful coincidence. Thank you both so much," she said. "Absolute best birthday presents ever."

After Adam left, Meghan insisted, not for the first time, that her brother and I ought to be better friends. "Do you need more proof than the gifts you just gave me? You think alike, you're both bibliomaniacs, both a little reclusive, and both a bit nuts, just like me," she said, as we washed and dried dishes.

When she retired to the bathroom to get ready for bed, I furtively took a look at the autograph in Adam's gift. I don't suppose I should have been irked to see that it was a somewhat admirably executed forgery, or so it seemed in the candlelight, but it galled me nonetheless. I, who could have done a better job of it, had gone out and tracked down an authentic signed Yeats, while this was all her vaunted brother could manage? Naturally, I had no intention of telling her. My soul may at times be dirty, but it's not diabolical. She was happy and that made me happy. But that night solidified my feelings toward Adam. My purpose henceforth was to be outwardly nice toward him whenever he and I were thrown together, but otherwise stay as far away from the man as I could. He set my teeth on edge, let me admit it, and I didn't like feeling that way. Meantime, Henry James's letters to me persisted, sporadic and damning.

"You all right?" Meghan asked, startling me from my unpleasant reverie.

"Oh, I'm sorry," snapping to as the luncheon was breaking up. "Thinking about Adam is all."

She smiled, sadly. "What were you thinking?"

"About that time when we both gave you those signed Yeats books."

As I helped her on with her coat before heading out to the car, she said, with aching wistfulness, "Those are my two favorite possessions in the world."

Outside, the clouds had let forth with fine ice pellets that stung our faces like arctic nettles, making me marvel what a crummy world it is we sometimes inhabit.

MY DOWNFALL CAME on an otherwise classically beautiful autumn day. I was in my apartment making coffee after sleeping in. Meghan and I had been out the night before on one of our subway excursions to an outer borough neighborhood for some lamb curry she'd read was the best in the city, and I had gotten home late after dropping her off at her place. The knocks at my door came in three insistent bursts, like nothing any of my neighbors would ever make. I hitched my bathrobe tight, finger-combed my hair, and walked to answer, my stomach churning. The letters promised this moment, and I sensed it was now upon me. Two men stood there, one of medium height and artificially tanned, the other stocky and short with pockmarks on his cheeks, each displaying a badge and looking past me into the room. I had seen such things in movies but it was surreal, to say the least, for it to transpire before my very eyes, and not in some darkened theater but my own home.

There is no need to describe in detail what happened next, given it was all more or less as one might expect. A typical investigation had gone on for several months, one in which I was drawn into selling a couple of overpriced forgeries to a couple of second-tier dealers I would never speak to again, nor they to me. One of the books was a relatively inconsequential Robert Frost, but the other, a signed copy of *Dubliners* dated 1914, the year of publication—my rendering of James Joyce's signature running upward from left to right as was his sometime habit—was a different story. Big money, that one, well into five figures. Some overpriced, overrated autograph experts were brought in to verify what the police wanted to hear, and thus was I stung.

The only freakish part about the arrest was that the officers, who came in and sat with me to talk a little before making their collar, provided me with a copy of a confession to my crimes written out in *my own hand*— yes, I do have my own personal handwriting, and much as we are let down when an impersonator speaks in his regular voice, my penmanship left a few things to be desired. They didn't seem to like it when, seeing words I hadn't written right there in my own hand, I let out with a loud, thunderstruck laugh. Of course, I thought. Whoever had been sending me the menacing letters in James's hand could not resist a pièce de résistance, an inside joke only he and I would truly appreciate. Even as I spent the night downtown sitting on the hard concrete bench of a holding cell with twenty other miscreants until being released on my own recognizance the next morning, I vacillated between hating the bastard who did this to me and admiring his sense of humor. The counterfeit of my handwriting wasn't perfect, which led me to infer that my accuser worked up his facsimile from fragments he hadn't spent much time studying or else wasn't all that accomplished. Still, the resemblance was close enough that it would have taken someone with my skill to recognize it as a forgery, and on this neither the police nor courts would ever accept my considered testimony—if it ever came to that, which it didn't.

Too, I began racking my brain, going through the many hundreds of deals I had been involved in over the years, trying to figure out who was behind my sudden shift of fortune. I should add that Adam Diehl, right or wrong, was on my short list. He for one would have had access to my handwriting if he'd secretly read my letters to Meghan, of which there were quite a number, as we shamelessly adored penning each other private love notes, especially in our earliest months of dating. Stealing glances at our romantic exchanges wouldn't have been hard for Adam to do, since whenever he visited town he stayed at her place while she moved over to mine. On the other hand, because I was an avowed Luddite who stubbornly refused to deal with computers, any number of other letters, not to mention invoices and checks, were out there in the bibliophilic universe for someone to study and mimic.

Now let me say in no uncertain terms that a night in jail, especially in the jail known as the Tombs in lower Manhattan, is one night too many. Not knowing whether I faced more than just that one, I resolved to do everything within my now somewhat constrained powers to make things right, to pay the myriad pipers and try to resuscitate my life. Meghan was crucial in this process.

"You have such amazing knowledge and skill," she assured me. "It's only a matter of putting them to work in ways that benefit not you but others."

Inspirational words, though I had to admit to myself, and myself only, that somewhere along the line I had evolved a deluded, fanciful, and finally illicit conceit that my work *did* benefit others by bringing the beauty of previously unwritten words and ideas into the world. Pure narcissism, I guess, in the end. Not the kind of philosophy that would aid in marching me out of the financial, legal, and ethical bog into which I had slid— or, rather, been slyly thrust.

One of my first calls was to my Providence colleague, who had already heard about it down the lightning-quick rare book grapevine. My incarceration wasn't, thank heavens, glamorous or significant enough to make the news, but dealers are born information junkies and as given to gossip as any smallish, specialized community out there.

"I have to admit," Atticus scolded, "there were moments I suspected you of something like this. They were far and few between, mind you, but once in a while a book or letter was so exceptional that, well, I wondered. Then I always remembered your father and told myself that an apple can't fall that far from the tree. Especially such a great tree as he was."

Yes, he was furious with me and also understandably hurt. I told him, truthfully, that quite a few of the things I had sold him over the years were genuine, mixed in with my admitted fabrications. Further, I said, sheepish in my new role as scoundrel, I would buy any and

everything back, plus, say, twenty percent—thirty—
for the trouble, no questions asked. I had always lived
rather modestly in my rent-controlled apartment and
cheap studio, with no expensive vices other than my
bibliophilia, and had built up a decent savings on top
of the money I'd inherited when my father had died,
money he wisely invested and I carefully maintained,
from which I could make restitutions. Too, I would dip
into my permanent collection—my now rather imper-
manent collection—and sell off some much-loved personal favorites in order to raise yet more money. All
I asked, pled for, in return was that he not press any
charges or sue me, to which he agreed.

To my deep relief, most others in the trade took a
similar approach to the situation, preferring to get their
money refunded over pursuing lawsuits and making
appearances in court. The police confiscated the fakes
that were removed from my apartment as well as collected from far and wide, and to this day I'm in the
dark about what happened to them, though I would
love to find out. My father had never harbored a deep
affection for the police and I suppose I followed in his
worthy footsteps in this regard. I enquired, more than
once, but was told by my probation officer to drop the
matter. The less said, the better, he advised me. The
thing is, I continued to think my handiworks were in-
trinsically valuable whereas in the eyes of the law they
were utterly worthless. Still, an enterprising member
of the force with access to confiscated materials might
sensibly agree with my assessment and spirit away a
volume or three or ten, unnoticed over time, and quietly get them back out into the market. I could just hear
him describing them to a secondhand bookseller, my

phantom dirty cop. "We found these in my grandma's house when she died, guess my grandfather had been a collector back in the day, don't know what they're worth but my family's looking to sell them." The secondhand dealer buys them on the low side and calls another dealer a bit higher up in the hierarchy, says he picked up some nice things over the transom, and flips the books for a profit. Assuming the next dealer was unaware of their tarnished provenance, he or she marks them to full retail value and puts them up for sale. Who knows but that at some Armory show in the future my ostracized children will begin to resurface, one by one?

As might be expected, Meghan's friends and some of the customers at her shop with whom she was close expressed concern about my trustworthiness, whether or not it would hurt her own reputation as a bookseller to remain involved with me, and god knows what other criticisms. These irreproachable bastions of sinless good, for all their dire efforts to save Meghan from my destructive self, were, I'm relieved to report, hopelessly out of touch with just how close we were. My mistake, my crime, my being outed weren't going to shatter our love any more than if she did something similarly wrong. If anything, my trials, as it were, opened up deeper avenues of love than we might otherwise have traveled. While I couldn't fairly fault her confidantes—I *was* the "author" of my own troubles—it didn't mean they failed to irritate me with their pious, holier-than-thou meddling. Still, as I say, this was predictable and mundane.

What was not predictable was Adam's solicitude. Was he supportive of me and Meghan because he knew that I knew about him, dreaded I might sink some accusatory talons into the soft underbelly of his quack ventures and drag him down with me, out of the forgers' firmament? Did he quietly admire my resilient refusal to let this ruin me? Had he finally found it in himself to stop being rankled about my relationship with his sister, one that forced him to share her time and affection?—never to forget, they were orphans from early on. Maybe, doubtful, and absolutely not were the answers to these questions. Still, despite snippets of overheard—and admittedly, one time, eavesdropped—phone conversations Meghan had with her brother in which it was clear he wished she would find herself another boyfriend, he seemed more sorry for me than triumphant.

Over time, fortunately, just as her meddlesome friends moved on to offer their prudent advice about the sins of others among their acquaintance, Adam slowly withdrew back into his own ascetic life in Montauk. These developments came as equal relief. My brief jail time and long days of sweeping cigarette butts, dead leaves, used condoms, and the like in city parks and along median strips of avenues, fulfilling my obligatory community service hours one full contractor's bag at a time, did finally come to an end. After being turned down at a number of establishments, I was finally hired at a small but distinguished auction house. My new employer had known me before on a casual basis and had always admired my expertise in literary and political autograph materials from a distance, heard good things about me. Thank heavens I had never consigned any of my handiwork in his rooms, so my slate was clean. The probationary terms he set were plain, simple, and I thought very doable: *Don't mess up.*

Mess up I didn't. I arrived on time daily and went straight to my cataloguing desk, where I researched and wrote bibliographic descriptions of a host of books and manuscripts in my preferred field of late-nineteenth- and early-twentieth-century British and American rarities. By not being in the business of buying or selling any items myself, I was able to use my years of expertise to examine and describe others' holdings and steer entirely clear of any personal involvement that would result in my being paid a penny more than my salary allotted. Oh, sure, I suppose I could have furtively snuck a signature into some book that had arrived unsigned at the auctioneer's. But I would easily have gotten caught. Too many people in our offices, for one, and besides, the consignor would know. There was no specific profit in cataloguing, which provided me with a truly safe work environment to regain my place in society. If I didn't feel the giddy, almost ecstatic pleasure of forgery, I was rewarded most every day by a sensation of mellow happiness, the serenity that comes from conducting oneself honestly, on the up and up.

FEBRUARY SNOW AND MARCH SLEET gave way to April rain and May sunshine, and still no arrest had been made in Adam's death. To say this frustrated Meghan would be an understatement. As for myself, I suppose I had read too many Conan Doyle stories in which Holmes deduces his path to the killer, quoting Tacitus's epigram *"Omne ignotum pro magnifico"*—everything unknown is wonderful—as he goes, doing his drugs and gently teasing Watson while puffing his pipe, not to be underwhelmed by the investigators' failure to find their man. That Adam had knowingly sold ersatz signatures and documents would necessarily have exposed him to some very outraged, even enraged buyers—were they made aware of his counterfeiting exploits—over the years. Just ask me; I know. And yet who in their right mind would be angry enough to kill, assuming it was Adam's forgeries that got him into trouble?

As it happened, he was not as good at keeping records over the years as I had always been. If my meticulous records made any plausible deniability impossible during my own time afoul the law, Adam Diehl's lack thereof ironically protected the identity of some of those who might possibly have had a hand in denying him his life. So unless clients stepped forward demanding money back for items he had sold to them, and curiously few did, there was no money trail to follow. What was more, the messy crime scene in the Montauk bungalow never turned up any very usable forensics, which didn't help matters, either. It did come out, to Meghan's discouragement, that the first officers to arrive contaminated quite a bit of evidence by ham-handedly, if not ham-footedly, going through the bungalow, stepping on books and blood, their guns drawn in case a bad guy still lurked on the premises. So, with the search stymied and most manpower reallocated, the scent lost if there ever was one, Adam's murder moved closer and closer to a cold case file.

It had been bittersweet when the police informed Meghan that they had done everything necessary toward completion of their work at the bungalow, and she could feel free to access the house whenever she liked. Bitter because it underscored the investigation's having come to a vague, no, realistic if incomplete kind of end. Sweet, if sweet it could be called, because the Diehl cottage was still a beautiful, sentimentally rich place in Meghan's view, despite its recent gruesome history. Pleasure-filled memories of childhood and of good times with Adam in later adult years centered on Montauk, and with my help she was going to do her best to see whether positive memories might not overcome the bad. If it proved impossible—and it well might, given she had lost her entire family in or near the prime oceanfront property—we agreed that Meghan would offer it up for sale. Montauk beachfront land is golden, and a conservative estimate would put the bungalow in the low seven figures, far more than enough for us to make a fresh start together somewhere else if we wanted. We even discussed taking a few months off from our work in New York, perhaps splurging on a rental somewhere warm—in the south of France or the Italian Riviera, maybe. It wasn't as if our first years together hadn't been tested by problems. A clean break from trials and tragedies might be the best medicine.

One evening after work, Meghan surprised me.

"Let's go to Montauk," she said out of the blue. "I think I'm finally ready."

I hesitated, asked, "You're sure?" wondering if she was truly prepared to visit the site of her brother's slaughter.

"I'm sure of it," she replied. "In fact, I'd like to go first thing tomorrow if you're free. It's a Saturday, supposed to be nice weather. The staff can run the shop. There's no need to put this off another day."

We rose predawn, quickly packed a picnic lunch, drove through the Midtown Tunnel to the Long Island Expressway and on toward Montauk. Sipping coffee from a Thermos, we watched a flat orange sun fatten, round, and rise into a flawless morning sky. The traffic at that hour was light and we made good time. When I pulled off the highway, the sun was fully up, the joggers

and dog walkers were about, and soon enough we rolled
into the short lane that led to the bungalow.

"Would you like to stretch your legs first, take a
stroll on the beach?"

Knowing that in my reluctant way I was hoping to
mitigate the trauma of being here, Meghan turned to
me with a grateful smile, said, "We can, afterward. Let's
do this while I still have the nerve."

We were surprised to see that yellow police tape still
crisscrossed the front door.

Turning to Meghan, I asked, "Wasn't the investigation all wrapped up here?"

"That's what they told me."

"Probably just forgot to remove the tape, but maybe
we should leave it alone. There another door?"

"Around back facing the water."

I followed her along the side of the cottage past
thorny barberry bushes that looked not to have been
trimmed for years, downhill on a narrow private path
past heavy pilings supporting a cantilevered porch that
overlooked the panorama of pristine beach. We climbed
a flight of uneven stairs set partly into the hillside leading up from the sand. The rhythmic roar and whoosh
of the waves was punctuated by gulls squawking as they
soared, much like kites on unseen strings, above our
heads. On the deck, a couple of weatherworn wooden
chairs, paint peeling, lay on their sides. We righted
them, then walked to the back door whose screen was
ajar, clapping anxiously in the skittish breeze. Clear as
the sky was, a fine mist off the rollers gave the air a rich,
salty fragrance as it dampened our skin.

I stood aside so Meghan could go in first. The
odor inside was awful: sterile yet tainted, musty and

chemical-acrid. We pulled up the window shades that
faced onto the deck and Atlantic horizon beyond and
opened the windows to let in some fresh sea air. Without saying a word, looking around the suddenly sun-
flooded room, I knew we were both relieved to see that
few signs of the chaos left behind in Adam's studio were
visible. A mitigation crew had come in and removed
anything biologically hazardous, which meant they had
mopped the hardwood of dried blood, steamed the
carpets, washed the walls, and so forth. The vandalized
items and other miscellanea relevant to the crime had
since been photographed and removed to a lab where
no doubt they would remain in storage until the per-
petrator had been caught, charges brought, and Adam's
ruined stuff submitted as evidence.

"For some reason I didn't expect them to have left
behind any of his books," Meghan said, walking to the
shelves that lined the walls and randomly pulling one
down.

"I'm glad they did," I said, following her. "I guess
these weren't useful to the cops so they're all yours
now. Everything here is," I continued, squinting at an
Augustus John drawing in a vintage gilt frame over
Diehl's desk. It appeared to be quite genuine, not that
I knew or even sensed that he might have been into fin
de siècle art forgery.

Meghan handed me the book she held, a bright
dust-jacketed copy of Carl Sandburg's *The American
Songbag*, signed on the front endpaper. "Is it?"

I looked at the copyright page, 1927. "Is it a first edition? Yes."

"No, no, please. Is it real?"

"The autograph?"

She frowned with obliging impatience as I turned back to the signature, knowing that she knew that I knew what she'd meant. The look on her face was apprehensive, hopeful, serious. I studied it, having decided what my answer would be whether or not the autograph was forged.

To my delight, it sang with authenticity. Sandburg's wide-nibbed fountain pen was evident, as were his Yankee legibility and baseline as level and straight as a schoolmarm's ruler. The garlanded "db" ligature in his surname made it look as if the poet had dropped a whimsical, curlicued "M" smack dab in the middle of "Sandburg." All of it was, blessedly, and not to mention surprisingly, correct.

"Right as rain," I assured her.

A random search through the flyleaves and title pages of a number of other books often produced the same happy outcome. The first editions were first editions. The condition was uniformly solid. Most of the authorial inscriptions were right, so far as I could tell on the spot without doing any research, and those that weren't I simply kept to myself. Meghan's pale face was aglow, rosy as a Homeric dawn with relief. Not because she had inherited a valuable collection of literary rarities but because, however unsalvageably ruined as he himself might have been, Adam's reputation was, to her mind, very much rehabilitated. He was not entirely a fraud, and these books on the shelves of the house where he had spent the last years of his life proved it. His bibliographic knowledge seemed estimable, and while his collection was quirky—a more flat-footed collector would have doggedly assembled a wall of standard, canon-approved titles—it showed character. Why he would bother to mix in forgeries of his own making, given they were often subpar, with genuine works was beyond me. Who was he kidding? Not himself and not me.

Strange fellow, I thought, then asked, "While we're at the authentication game, what about that Augustus John drawing? You're the art afficionado here."

Without even looking at it, she said, "It better be right. My grandfather on my father's side bought it from John's nephew in the old country, and it's been in the family for decades. Isn't it beautiful?"

It was beautiful. A sensual portrait of a Pre-Raphaelite belle, chin lightly perched on her wrist as her frank gaze met the viewer directly in the eye. Admiring the deftness of the artist's pencil, touched by the story of the drawing's provenance and its being passed down from generation to generation in Meghan's family, I felt a sudden ache of regret, of sadness, of disgust that people such as myself and the late Adam Diehl would deign to falsify objects as exquisite as this drawing. Yet we did. Just as perhaps someone a century or so ago might have faked this very image that Meg and I were now admiring. We did so not merely because we could but because our own passions, skewed according to society's dictates, led us to do it. Our passions may be different from what Augustus John felt toward his female model, with whom he had clearly been in love, but were borne of masterful skill and inspiration nevertheless.

It was a confounding moment, my thoughts reeling as I pictured the violent scene that had occurred in this very room. None of it seemed real. But then the "real" never did much for me, I must admit. I understood just then that, finally, the greatest difference between Meghan's brother and her lover was—with the curious exception of that Conan Doyle cache I bought from Atticus Moore—just this. Whereas he copied, I created. Whereas he was an artisan, I was an artist. But whereas he was dead without further recourse, I felt myself in a limbo. If I could draw with the mastery of Augustus John but was not Augustus John, why should I deny myself the chance to capture his experience of making this drawing, or one akin, or words possibly even better? I remembered something the greatest art forger of the twentieth century, Elmyr de Hory, once said about his canvases, that if you hang them in a museum with a collection of great paintings, and if they hang there long enough, they become real. He was a true believer.

"Are you all right?" Meghan was asking me.

"Fine, fine," I said, pulling myself together. "Too much coffee," and smiled at her, although as long as I live I will never forget the quick vertigo I felt at that moment, posing a question that had no answer for me.

Meghan and I continued to examine books from Adam's library. Most of them were signed or inscribed, a mishmash of famous titles and items more of personal interest, none alphabetized or even arranged by subject. An eccentric's athenaeum. An autographed copy of *Bleak House* was shelved next to a history of Scottish equestrians. Several William Faulkners with signatures that looked wrong to me—Faulkner is the darling of amateur forgers because he looks so easy to fake, although in fact he's extremely hard—I found alongside a treatise by the Russian esotericist and mathematician P. D. Ouspensky, whose signature I neither knew nor cared about. Again and again the question of authenticity arose, sometimes Meghan asking, other times me exclaiming because again and again many of the signatures and inscriptions were, when within my purview of knowledge, authentic. Those that weren't, weren't, not that I felt it necessary, at least at that moment, to divulge the fact to Meghan.

We took a break to eat our lunch on the beach. Sandwiches, chips, white wine in plastic cups. The sky was immaculate, every cloud swept beyond the edges of the horizon, so that we sat on our beach blanket beneath a perfect dome of cerulean. The sea breeze played through Meghan's hair and at that moment I felt I'd never seen her looking so lovely.

"You glad we came?" I asked.

"There's nothing about this that's easy or at all what you'd call fun, but yes, I am glad we came. Maybe it's a first baby step toward getting things straightened out in my head."

"Closure, you mean?"

"I doubt I'll ever have closure, the way he died. But I mean, just trying to understand what really happened, get a better sense of what's real and what isn't."

There was that knotty word again, *real*.

"You said you wanted to go through his papers, bills and things, before we head back?" I asked, moving us away from the subject as we gathered our things and folded the blanket.

"The lawyer says it's necessary to get the estate in order."

Back up at the cottage we divided tasks. I volunteered to go through what there was of his bookseller accounts, see if there were any outstanding invoices that needed to be settled and, as well, if he was owed money by anyone in the trade. Meghan would attend to utility bills and the like.

His bookseller files were, I had to believe, even messier than I think Adam himself had kept them. The investigators had rifled through these documents and returned them in a couple of bankers boxes, having found either nothing useful or something of interest they'd followed up on with no result. A couple of invoices did appear to need payment. These I set aside. I felt compelled, for reasons that escape me, to reorganize the files chronologically, put them back the way I thought they should go by year, month, bookseller name. It was meditative, I suppose, and I'd had just enough of the wine and ocean air to feel a mellow serenity settle over me even in the midst of such a curious and in many ways awful task.

Then I came upon a document that snatched my breath away. A typewritten invoice for a clutch of seventeen unpublished letters by Arthur Conan Doyle pertaining to *The Hound of the Baskervilles* together with a manuscript fragment from the same work. What? The seller's name on the rather amateurish invoice, torn out of one of those generic pads that anyone could purchase from a stationer's shop, was not one I recognized. Or, no, I did. Henry Slader. This had to be the same person the police had mentioned. The address was Dobbs Ferry, a leafy hamlet a short distance up the Hudson from New York. No date or any indication whether Diehl had paid, though I assumed he had since there appeared to be no follow-up notices. On the back of the invoice was a column of numbers, handwritten in pencil, that I couldn't interpret other than to guess that they might represent further debts. I was stunned, stupefied. This suggested—no, it *meant* that Adam Diehl had not forged the cache of documents that I had so admired, envied, and, I must admit, even hated him at times for having conceived and brought into being. I glanced at Meghan, who was poring over bills at another table at the far end of the studio, and, seeing that she was focused on her task, silently folded the bill and slipped it into my pants pocket. Whoever this Slader was, I intended to find out. As we drove back to the city that evening, Meghan asked me why I was so quiet.

"Just thinking about how lives can get so complicated in ways we don't have much control over. Adam's, I mean."

"Well, I'm sorry he's not around to complicate life any more," she said, wistful, looking at the Patek Philippe, which she had secured loosely around her wrist, tightening its buckle as far as it would go.

He is, though, I thought, as I reached over and squeezed her hand.

DOBBS FERRY IS KIND OF a riverside version of Montauk, at least in the sense that Manhattan is so proximate and yet feels light-years away. Having taken the day off from work and telling Meghan I wanted to do some solo book scouting—there are very good shops in the area with shelves bowing under the weight of first editions, and I needed to take a break—I drove up the Saw Mill River Parkway, turned off at the exit I'd looked up earlier, and found my way to the address listed on Henry Slader's invoice. I had already tried to look him up in both dealer directories and the phone book but didn't find him listed. Admittedly, I wasn't surprised by his absence from the grid but did have to wonder why in the world he would have provided Adam with an invoice in the first place rather than make a cash deal for the Sherlock Holmes archive, sidestep the paperwork, and call it a day. A banner day at that.

As I pulled onto the street, I felt both foolish—some faux private eye on his first stakeout—and unnerved—what was I going to do if I did locate Henry Slader? Ask him if perchance he had a lost Sherlock tale lying around the workroom? It was a residential lane, more suburban than rural, with neat houses up and down the block flanked by mature chestnut, oak, and maple trees in full June glory and green, green grass. Meant he worked at home, just as I did once upon a time. I brought my car to a stop across the street from a modest red brick, two-story house. Oddly, or at least unexpectedly, some children's toys were scattered about on the lawn—a pink foam soccer ball, a small bicycle lying on its side, colorful plastic tassels dangling from the handlebar butts. Other than this evidence of liveliness, the stodgy facade of the house, with its black front door centered between two windows, shades half-drawn, looked like a man lost in slumber. Before climbing out of the car to go knock on that dark door, I hesitated, wondering if I really, truly wanted to awaken the sleeper. It wasn't as if I knew what I was going to ask or say, although I had toured through all kinds of scenarios in my head over the days and nights after Meghan and I returned from Montauk. How did you know Adam? What else did you sell him? How did you ever manage to pull off that splendid Baskerville fabrication? Who the hell are you?

The woman who opened the door was too old to be the mother of young children. White hair tucked up into a loose bun, a wrinkled royal blue housedress. Of all things, she pressed a ball of tissue paper to her left nostril. "Can I help you with something?"

Swallowing back my disconcertment at her nose-bleed, I said, "I'm looking for Henry Slader," peering past her into the foyer. "He lives here, right?"

"Did. I rented him an apartment at the back of the house. But he left a couple months ago. If you know him, I got mail for him."

Here I hesitated. This was a line probably not to be crossed, although I wanted to say, Yes, thanks, I'll get it to him. She could easily have caught me out on such a schoolboy ruse, however, and I half-wondered if her easy offer wasn't a setup. "I know someone who knew him, my girlfriend's brother."

"Well, I'm sorry but I can't help you. I have no idea where he went or I'd forward him his mail."

"Would you happen to remember if an Adam Diehl ever visited him? Tallish guy with red hair, book collector."

She needed no time to consider the question. "He never had no visitors, except for some police who wanted to ask him about something out in Long Island. He didn't know nothing about it, was what he said. So I'm sorry but—" and she lifted away the bloodied tissue, frowned at it, shrugged, and sighed. "I wish I could help you but I'm afraid I can't."

"Mom, what is it?" a woman in her thirties asked, appearing abruptly by her side in the doorway with a young boy, clearly the owner of the ball and bike, in tow.

"This gentleman is looking for Mr. Slader."

"Oh," she said, as the boy pressed past her and my-self, heading for the front yard to play. "We have some mail of his. Mostly catalogues it looks like."

Without a thought, I leapt on this unexpected second chance. "I was telling your mother here that my girlfriend's brother knows him and—"

"Great," she said, disappeared for a moment while the boy's grandmother and I, each of us distracted, watched him kick his soccer ball around.

As I drove back to the city, I realized my purloined invoice might simply have been one among others the authorities had found, followed up on, and deemed too insubstantial to pursue further. Had they known—how could they have?—that the Baskerville letters were not what they appeared to be, they might have looked into it further. They didn't, but I had to. At the same time, I quarreled with myself about having taken Slader's mail. The vague claim I would try to get it to him was so obviously specious—why would I come looking for him in Dobbs Ferry if I knew where he was?—that I was embarrassed for his landlady and her daughter when they accepted my offer. But I couldn't help myself. The catalogues and a couple of letters sat next to me on the passenger seat, accusatory, yes, but also promising. Enough illegitimacy seemed to hover, like thick blinding fog, around Henry Slader that I knew these were my only hope of figuring out his story. Paranoid, I kept glancing in the rearview mirror expecting to see revolving bright lights atop a squad car, the landlady in the front seat pointing her finger at me, the forging, mail-thieving felon, as the police bore down. Patent lunacy, to be sure. I would never see those people again in my life.

Back in my apartment that afternoon, I opened the letters first. To my dismay, both were of the uselessly anonymous To Whom It May Concern variety. Discouraged, I next tore open the envelopes of the three antiquarian bookseller catalogues. These were a bit more auspicious. Two of the dealers were well established—indeed, I had already received both offerings in the mail some while back—but the other, from Pennsylvania, wasn't known to me. That wasn't altogether unusual, as the world is full of part-time dabblers in the trade, well-meaning decent book people who vend their stuff on-line and at rural fairs, who display secondhand volumes in the back of antique stores or in book barns, who keep their stock in dry basements or spare bedrooms. The book world was a crazy quilt of devotees who often shared little else than a rabid passion for the printed page. I couldn't, and didn't, know every bookseller out there, not by a thousand country miles.

My two known contacts, both in New York City, were kind enough to look up their current customer information for Slader, only to find that he had not up-dated his address beyond Dobbs Ferry. My excuse for asking was reasonable, as I told them I owed him some money and couldn't locate him. They had no better idea where he was than I did. One quipped, "Wish every customer we've got was as diligent about their bills as you." Rather than approach the Pennsylvania dealer, who didn't know me from, well, Adam, I called Atticus, with whom I had gone through the excruciating fire of apology, restitution, and slow deliberate reconciliation, and now enjoyed as close a friendship as a somewhat wary forgiveness allowed. His reply fascinated me.

"He shares some of your same interests, back when you were selling and buying."

"I still buy," I countered. "I just don't sell anymore."

"Well, he sells more than buys. Or used to. Hasn't been around for a while."

While I digested what he'd said, the silence must have been telling, as his tone of voice changed when he asked me if there was something regarding Henry Slader he needed to worry about.

Assuring him that Slader wasn't anyone to concern himself with, I explained that Meghan and I had gone through her brother's papers a couple of weeks ago and we found something there from him that needed to be addressed, is all.

"Just trying to tie up whatever loose ends on the estate that we can."

"They solve the murder?"

"Not yet," I said.

"That's crazy. You're a Sherlock Holmes man, must drive you up the wall that there aren't his kind around these days to make things right. Not to mention poor Meghan Diehl."

Feeling more like Professor Moriarty than Mr. Holmes, I thanked him and rang off.

As for the Pennsylvania dealer, I telephoned and attempted to order a couple of books that I imagined, based on what I had just learned, might be in Slader's taste. Both were already sold. I desperately wanted to ask who bought them but realized I had reached a hard stone wall at the end of this particular path in the maze. I was stymied. When the dealer, not recognizing my voice, asked if I was on his mailing list for future catalogues, I said, Thanks, no, and hung up. My trip to Dobbs Ferry, my pathetic little theft, my hopeful, fibbing phone calls—all of it was for naught. Even after dinner that night, when Meghan asked me to show her the books I had scored on my Hudson Valley pilgrimage, I had to admit the trip was a bust.

"Not a single book? That's so unlike you," she said.

"I guess I'm too distracted right now to think about buying books."

"But I thought that was part of the idea for going. Get your mind off things."

"Well, it didn't work, I'm afraid."

Why I kept the truth from her, I couldn't say in so many words. It was, as the phrase has it, a gut decision. In point of fact, I knew Henry Slader only somewhat less than Adam Diehl, intimately connected to me as I intuited they each were, and in ways beyond my seemingly paltry comprehension.

IN THE MONTHS AFTER that fruitless visit to Dobbs Ferry, I began to slip into what others might view as a mild, general depression but what I saw basically as a desperate defeat that came from being divided from what I loved. I am not, of course, referring to Meghan, whom I adored and who returned my love daily with great devotion, patience, and kindness. Indeed, it was Meghan who, on seeing my mood swing more often into the darker registers as the months moved on through autumn into early winter, asked me if we might not want to go away, get out of the city and our routines, finally take that trip to Italy we had been talking about, or the Caribbean, somewhere warm for Christmas.

I thought, Why not? My work at the auction house had clicked into a coglike routine, and although I liked working with all the inscribed books and various documents, gained lots of new knowledge by being proximate to so many historically interesting materials, a routine was a routine, devoid of risk, of adventure, of anything that made my heart quicken. I was lucky to have a job, I knew, but it was just and only that, a job rather than a calling. Any hopes I might have had about locating and possibly confronting Henry Slader had dwindled away so swiftly that at times he seemed more a mirage or dream than an actual person out there somewhere, living and breathing and fencing fakes, sometimes flawed, other times exquisite, to other unsuspecting Adam Diehls of the world. Slader was, I had to admit, a dead end. It was healthiest for me to forget about the man. I could have gone to the police with my suspicions about him but, first, they were merely suspicions extrapolated from an old invoice for some forged Sherlock Holmes papers, which were now, innocently yet damningly, in my possession. And second, perhaps more important, I'd had enough of cops, thank you, and worried my action would one way or another come back to haunt me. So I told Meghan that, yes, getting out of New York for the holidays was a great idea. I left the decision up to her as to where we would go and she surprised me by reserving tickets not for the Italian coast or the French Riviera or even the Caribbean, but her birthplace, Ireland—a direct flight to Dublin.

"Sure, it'll be chilly, but we can bundle up. You know I've been longing to go. And besides, you like manuscripts so much, I thought it was high time you get to see the finest one of them all."

I pondered for a moment, ticking through the pantheon of Irish writers from the last couple hundred

years, then realized she had in mind something far earlier, the ninth century.

"Trinity College? The Book of Kells. You're brilliant,"
I said, genuinely moved by her thoughtfulness. For anyone interested in the highest calligraphic arts, in the
illuminated manuscript lifted to the level of pure divin-
ity, the Book of Kells was the ultimate lodestone desti-
nation. I had owned a handsome folio facsimile edition
since my teens, when my parents had given it to me for
my birthday. Now I would see the real thing.

"And for me," Meghan added, "a pilgrimage over to
Drumcliff and Yeats's grave will do just fine."

"Not to mention a couple of pints in Sligo Town. All
perfect. Better than perfect."

As the time drew closer for our trip, my mood did
brighten even though the reason for my periodic dejec-
tion remained very much in place, a fault—for it was a
fault, and all of my own doing—I tried my best to hide.

You see, I must make another confession in order
to clarify. Addiction is always stronger than the addict.
Or at least my addiction was. The degradation of arrest, all the attendant humiliations that followed, the
loss of so many friends in the book trade, the long daily
grinding journey back into society—none of these, each
of which convulsed through my life like a merciless
hurricane, deterred my eventual return to the forger's
art. Even my lemons-into-lemonade resurrection as a
legitimate handwriting expert and scholarly cataloguer
couldn't save me from my truer self. It was probably my
love for Meghan that held me back from a complete
reversion to form, sweet Meghan who had remained at
my side throughout the entire season of hell and even
now, despite her own loss, was protective of me. But

alone in the evening, left to my own devices, I found myself practicing, writing out some cherished Thomas Hardy poems in the master's hand, penning Churchill's famous "We shall fight on the beaches . . . we shall fight in the fields and in the streets . . . we shall never surrender" speech in Sir Winston's script, and of course conjuring some will-o'-the-wisp Conan Doyle notes toward a "lost" essay in which he confesses to being the mastermind behind the Piltdown Man forgery. This latter was an idea I had toyed around with since my early twenties, when I first learned about the Piltdown hoax and theories that once abounded connecting Sherlock Holmes's creator to it. He was, after all, a retired doctor and amateur archaeologist who collected old bones, and he certainly had the necessary knowledge as well as shrewd brilliance to pull off such a convincing stunt. Mine was as good an idea as the Piltdowner's himself, whoever he truly was.

Not without pangs of reluctance, I crumpled up these undeniably masterful doodlings and threw them out with the food scraps. Once stung, and all that. But forgery is as difficult a mistress to quit as she is to master, and before long I found myself keeping some of the finer examples for my own personal enjoyment. I knew I was but one step away from the garden path I'd already been down but trusted myself not to go that far. The sirens might be singing, to layer in another fine cliché, but I knew their song by heart and kept their invitation at bay.

Our trip, wonderful in every way and restorative to us each, lifted my obsession from me for the two weeks we were in Ireland from just before Christmas and into the New Year. Even when the weather was rainy and

wet chill wrapped itself around the very marrow of our
bones, we went about our tourist ways, visiting the famous Cliffs of Moher in the fog and St. Patrick's Cathe-
dral in the drizzle, and we were happy. And as for myself,
I was for a time dispossessed of even so much as thinking
about what to do regarding my recent tendencies toward
relapse. Because I had packed none of my writing implements or anything else necessary to create a forgery, I
couldn't have acted upon my impulses even if I'd wanted
to. No way meant no will. What was more, everyone here
was friendly, open, kind, and none of them—aside from
a couple of booksellers to whom I didn't introduce myself when Meghan and I visited their shops in Dublin
and Galway—had a clue or concern about who I was
and what I'd done in the past. I was a blank slate with
no shameful history and nothing to hide. I had forgotten how delicious anonymity was, especially the kind of
anonymity that involves not looking over one's shoulder.

On a particularly nasty night in a pretty lodge in Kenmare, on the southwest coast of the country, Meghan
and I were having dinner in the hotel restaurant as the
wind whipped against the windows and the sky lit up
now and then with silent lightning. We were nearing
the end of our vacation and were in an especially peaceful mood. A peat fire burned bright and warm, giving
off its earthen scent in the fireplace near our table, its
flames dancing on our claret glasses like animate spirits,
and without forethought or design I asked Meghan to
marry me.

"You sure that wine hasn't gone to your head?" she
teased, her eyes welling.

"I'm sure I want to marry you. What do you say?" I
told her, tightening my grasp of her hands on the table.

"I say 'Yes I said yes I will Yes.'"

"That's totally shameless, quoting Joyce in Ireland. A simple 'yes' will do."

"Then the answer's simply yes," and with that we reached across the table and kissed before signing for dinner and taking the unfinished bottle to our room upstairs.

Back in Manhattan, the aura of happiness did not dissipate. At least for a while. We were quietly married at City Hall downtown. Meghan's staff threw a lively reception for us at the bookshop, with homemade hors d'oeuvres and champagne, bouquets of white flowers that matched the snow delicately falling outside, and a carrot cake with raisins—Meghan's favorite—topped by a vintage kitschy plastic bride-and-groom statuette. Atticus even made the trek down and presented us with some high-end Irish whiskies wrapped in fancy foil—Green Spot, Connemara, Redbreast. Despite the bitter cold, the night was radiant. We walked home through fresh-fallen drifts of snow that muffled the usual sounds of the city and smoothed away its hard edges. Few others were out and about so late, and it felt as if we were among the last living beings in this fantastical white world.

Meghan and I decided that I would let my Gramercy apartment go as soon as the lease ran out and we would find a new place to live closer to Tompkins Square and the bookshop. My commute to the auction house wouldn't be all that much longer, and rents were a little more affordable in her neighborhood anyway. For the first time in many a year, life was good. We were making plans for the future and I was committed to staying on the straight and narrow. I was a husband now and must not backslide into venal, corrupt habits of the past, I warned myself. I could only hope, even pray, that some of my worst actions—ones that had up until then slipped beneath the waves of notice like some drowning man pulled from shore by riptides—would never resurface but wash away for good.

That said, I wasn't foolish or deluded enough to believe such a transient, fragile thing as happiness would last forever, and of course it didn't, but I cherished those times then and I cherish them even more now.

THE ONE-YEAR ANNIVERSARY of Adam's death promised to be a melancholy day. Yet I might never have guessed it to be the day on which a pestilent cloud that I thought had long since dispersed would abruptly throw me into dark, distressful shadow again. My anonymous correspondent—a man I had believed was dead, in fact murdered in Montauk and buried in a cemetery far enough from the ocean that his remains couldn't ever be wakened by the surf's sizzle and boom in stormy weather—resurfaced. Even though I was out of the forgery business, I received yet another threatening letter from some unhinged soul who must have missed the memo about my forced retirement and ongoing rehabilitation.

This time it was written to me in Arthur Conan Doyle's hand rather than Henry James's, which only made my anxiety deepen. Who on earth was this and what did he want? Whether it was Slader or somebody else, I represented no competition to him. Although I had years ago asked the police personally and through my lawyer to tell me who was behind the original series of letters and that bogus confession, they never divulged a name, insisting his identity wasn't known to them, either. They considered him an anonymous tipster and since, first, his information proved accurate and, second, there was no reward involved and, third, they had better things to do with their time, they were disinclined to pursue him.

Besides, they reminded me, they had not a shred of evidence that the accuser, skilled forger though he might have been, had ever used his talents to engage in any illegality, assuming he existed.

Assuming he existed? I asked them, incredulous.

Yes, assuming there had indeed been any forgeries involved beyond those brought into existence by your own hand.

So you people are saying I created these forged letters and sent them to myself in some psychotic, labyrinthine scheme to commit professional suicide?

Why not, was their response. They'd seen stranger.

These exchanges were infrequent, unpleasant, and fruitless. I believed strongly the police were protecting their source and, seeing no easy way around their blue wall, let the matter drop. I suppose there was a part of me that didn't finally want to know. Sometimes the stone unturned is best, I remember thinking.

But now he was back in all his pseudonymous glory. And what made his new letter even more vexing than any before was that its words replicated precisely those

in the very first letter I had received, initiating that original onslaught. *You shall be revealed,* it read. *Your decep-*
tions will prove you to be nothing more than a common
criminal & not the clever sophisticate you believe yourself
to be, and so forth.

Meghan noticed how agitated I was and in her in-
nocence marveled at how unhappy at Adam's grim anniversary I seemed to be. I weighed whether or not to
tell her, but our early married life had been so serene,
I dreaded that bringing her into what was clearly my
own private battle would cause more harm than good.
At the same time, she had proven herself to be such a
pillar of sanity that she might see something here that I
myself, blinded by worry, could not. I argued both possibilities without concluding anything.

On the weekend after receiving this letter, we made
our way out to Montauk to visit Adam's grave and toss
some stemmed roses into the ocean in his memory. Let
me admit, I who had never known fear, not really, was
now afraid. I found myself observing every stranger, especially men, with suspicion. Any of the mourners who
lingered at Fort Hill cemetery could have been posing.
It would not, after all, have taken a Sherlock Holmes
to predict that the late Adam Diehl's sister and now
brother-in-law would decide to pay homage on such
an important anniversary. We both had jobs, so a Saturday visit was logical. Having laid flowers at the base
of the headstone and flung more into the waves, we
made our way up the steps and into the bungalow to
set a bouquet on his empty desk. Meghan wept, and I
held her close to me, my heart beating hard and throat
tightening. After I handed her a glass of water, my every
gesture accomplished as if in slow motion, she asked

if I would mind giving her a few minutes alone in the cottage.

Out on the deck, I shivered a little. Not because it was cold. Indeed, the day was atypically warm for the season. No breeze, cirrus clouds above like ghostly fish bones. I watched a tanker edging its way across the horizon a dozen miles from shore and part of me wished I was aboard it, a crew member whose only vice was, say, a taste for drink, but was otherwise contentedly adrift on a toneless watery void.

Meghan joined me soon enough and slid her arm around my waist. She had stopped crying and offered me a brave smile, then gazed out at the Atlantic, too.

"I think the time has come to sell," she said. "There's nothing here for me any more. Nothing for either of us."

I couldn't disagree, but said, "You're sure about this."

"Never more sure of anything. Except marrying you, of course."

"Well, then, let's do it."

Wasting no time, we drove into the village to speak with a couple of realtors, settled on one who eagerly drove back to the property—for it was a "property" now—and, having given it a preliminary, cursory examination, agreed to appraise it, consult on the asking price, and put it up for sale. A contract was signed, duplicate keys handed over, and we promised to have the books and other effects removed as soon as possible. He advised us that the best season to sell would be spring or summer, but Meghan, having made her decision, was firm about listing it as soon as was feasible.

That night, back in the city, I marveled at my wife's ability to resolve on matters and make things happen. "It's a gift," I said, head turned on my pillow so I could see her profile in the faint ambient light from the streetlamps out the window.

"It's the orphan's imperative," was her response. "You learn it early because it's your only chance at survival."

"I love you," I whispered, my heart again beating so hard that my breath was shallow as a mindless dog's exhausted from running back and forth to fetch some meaningless stick. I needed to tell her my stalker, my epistolary nemesis was back, that he had never left, but just as I had lost what I loved the first time around, I was terrified that I would lose what I also loved, Meghan herself, this second go-around. If that happened there would be no surviving it, for I never learned the orphan's imperative or for that matter any other surefire survival skills that might assure me safe passage through this renewed provocation.

"I love you, too," she whispered back, then asked, "Why are you breathing so hard?"

"Desire," I half-lied but was blessed that I did because after we made love I fell into the deepest sleep I had experienced since our halcyon days in Eire.

The mail was my evening torture after work through the balance of February and March, but no further letters arrived. I began to wonder if that first one wasn't somehow a weird prank by the authorities, some arcane attempt to flush me out. It wasn't impossible, I reasoned with myself—no less credible than the possibility that I had sent myself those damning, damnable letters—given that the text was identical and they could surely locate someone skilled enough to make a passable forgery in Conan Doyle's hand. This was freakish wishful thinking, however, and I knew it. Paranoia makes for insane speculation much as insane speculation makes for terrible actions. I tried, therefore, not to act or even speculate.

April was here and Park Avenue's median gardens were teeming with red and yellow tulips. Meghan and I planned on attending the Armory show, having missed it last year because Adam's death was far too recent and raw and neither of us felt we could endure all the dealers' condolences and curiosity. We had accepted an offer on Montauk with buyers who met the asking price, were more than qualified for a loan, and didn't mind that a murder had taken place there because they intended to do a gut renovation. What furniture and other chattels failed to sell in an estate sale overseen by a local auction house were donated to a local hospice and a couple of other charities. The books were carefully boxed by Meghan's shop packer and put into storage. It was as if both a beloved remnant of personal history and a ruinous burden of tragic memories had broken free of their moorings and lifted away from the sandy coast into the aether. The world felt lighter, for a brief and welcome tenure, not just for my wife but for myself as well.

So mortifying was the second letter, which arrived a week before the book fair—*They may not know who killed Adam Diehl but I do*—that any impulse to tell Meghan I was under siege again was thwarted by the stomach-wrenching worry she might look at me with different eyes, eyes unduly suspicious. Not that this spectral madman could prove I had anything whatsoever to do with the death of her brother, this madman, I must say, who seemed more and more likely to be the elusive Henry Slader if only because he was the one person who could connect the various parties involved.

If it was him, he had to want something, surely, more substantial than just jarring my nerves. What was it? Ask, already, you bastard.

A follow-up letter the very next day both confirmed my suspicion and answered my angry, silent question. *I thank you for enquiring around about me a while ago. I have an enquiry now for you. You are in possession of materials that are rightfully mine*, it read. *Your pretty wife's brother saw fit to purchase that Baskerville archive from me, and bought a bunch of very valuable other things too, but never saw his way clear to finish paying for his pleasure. His untimely death brought an end to monthly payments he was making. I see you sold that nice beach house on the East End. In the interest of keeping things simple, let's say half of what you got for it, after agent commission of course, will just about satisfy Diehl's debt. That plus give me back the Baskerville archive & we can call ourselves even & nothing will happen. Revenge is a deadly enterprise as you know better than most.*

As before, no signature other than *A Conan Doyle* and no return address. I had no way to respond to either his statements or demands. Nor did I have any way of knowing whether his allegation that Adam had died owing him north of half a million dollars was a wild, delirious, wanton fabrication. While it was all well and good that he threatened to hang the blame for Adam's death on me—something the police never did—I noted that he himself had the motive if not the means, and had caught the investigators' attention, surely not without reason. Still, any thought of being accused of the murder of my wife's brother, any thought of facing the demeaning, debasing if not debased klieg lights of the criminal justice system, which as everyone knows has sent more than its unfair share of innocent people to prison, was beyond my ken. Unthinkable, untenable, impossible. Suicide was preferable to any prospect of reckoning minutes, days, months, years in a prison cell. No. Finally I had found happiness, the promise of a normal future, unclouded by torment, unstained by feelings of guilt. I wasn't going to let money, extorted or not, and some fraudulent Conan Doyle letters stand between me and my future with Meghan. If I wasn't reasoning with self-assurance, at least I was reasoning with what felt like pragmatism, or so I told myself as I charted my next move.

I telephoned Atticus and asked him if he had time to have lunch with me when he was in the city for the fair. "I have something private I need to ask, a favor," I said. "Don't worry, it's a favor that will benefit you, too."

"Why not just ask me on the phone?" I heard understandable and now somewhat familiar wariness in his voice, crackling like a partially spent fire at the edges of his words.

"I'd rather do it in person if that's all right. Day before the show opens?"

"All right. That nice French brasserie off Madison?"

We agreed on a time and I began that same evening inventorying what was left of my rare book collection—sadly somewhat decimated by the last time I needed to come up with money—including some of the better volumes from my father's library, which I had inherited and preserved with devotion, figuring that one day they might be passed down to my own son or daughter, were I ever fortunate enough to have one.

Not surprisingly, the figures added up quickly, but at the same time my conscience was torn in a chaos

of different directions. My father, as impeccable a collector as ever existed, would have died a second death
if he knew what I proposed to do to get myself out of
trouble. While amassing what in the trade are known as
"high spots"—famous books that influenced the course
of literary history—he specialized in Conan Doyle rarities, Sherlock Holmes having been his childhood hero
just as, no doubt directly encouraged by my father, he
had been my own. Like Holmes himself, my father had
a hawk nose and smoked a pipe. The man had been
genial among friends but was a razor-sharp, take-no-
prisoners defense attorney with an almost perfect track
record, who loved to refer jokingly to this case or that
as a two- or three-pipe problem. He would always go
the distance for you if you were fair, honest, and direct,
but if you misled or cheated him he had the instincts
of that hawkish nose of his and would hand you your
heart wrapped in butcher's paper and tied with a silk
ribbon.

What I considered a hundred-pipe problem my
father would simply have dismissed as empty threats
and undeserving of so much as pulling out the tobacco
pouch and pipe knife. But that was him, not me. And
what was more, if he witnessed me, with whom he had
shared the love of book collecting for so many years,
now proposing to bail myself out of this degenerate
mess of my own doing, would he have had any choice
other than to hand me my loathsome heart bundled up
in that butcher's paper? I realized I simply couldn't sell
off all of his life's joy, the last of his fond treasures from
my long-gone boyhood that I still possessed.

I made a decision. Negotiating a devil's pact with
myself, one forged from shame, I determined to keep

the highest of the high spots and—this made my chest
flutter, I'm sorry to acknowledge—"improve" many of
the lesser, though still quite desirable, volumes. It would
have to be the absolute finest work I had ever done, immaculate and utterly beyond question or reproach. I
would have to conceive and execute quickly, while Meg
was busy at the shop. Phoning work the next morning
after she had left, I announced, through a din of forced
coughs, that I'd been felled by a nasty cold and needed
to take some sick days. My boss said it was fine, feel
better. They had an auction coming up to coincide with
the Armory show, and my work on the catalogue was
long since done, anyway, so I wouldn't be missed.

My hand and eye behaved as if I were a decade
younger—agile, knowing, sure, deft, powerfully subtle—
and my conceits as to who the recipients of these generous inscriptions were in volume after volume showed
the maturity of one a decade older, so inventive were
they, extravagant yet inarguable in their plausibility.
The copies were already in exceptional condition, most
of them housed in quarter morocco clamshell boxes
and slipcases from earlier decades. And because my father, unlike many a more amateurish collector, rarely if
ever showed off his collection to others, nearly all of his
books—from Hawthorne to Twain, Wilde to Hammett,
and so on down the line—had been out of circulation
for a generation or more and, above all, had not been
seen since by anyone aside from myself. I was careful to
forge inscriptions and autographs only in first editions
of authors I was comfortable with while also trying to
work outside the canons of those authors with whom
I'd been associated when I was caught.

At lunch, over salad Niçoise and a carafe of Merlot, my head cold miraculously cured, I broached my
offer to Atticus. "Meghan and I have had such a rough
year that we've been talking about going overseas for
a while, traveling together a little, taking time off from
work and obligations and all the rest, and to cut a long
story short I've decided to sell my library, the good stuff,
the real stuff, obviously, along with much of my father's
library."

At the mention of my father's books, he became as
attentive as a cat cornering a mouse, or else a mouse
cornered by a cat.

"You know what a great collector he was," I added,
perhaps unnecessarily.

"You're prejudiced, but I've heard that said about
him many times over the years. He's a bit of a legend."

"Well, this is all in strictest confidence," I said
and seeing him nod, the look on his face serious and
thoughtful, continued. "After that nasty business some
years ago about the forging and all, I was pretty wiped
out financially. Work at the auction house only pays so
much. Meghan sold off the family house in Montauk
for a sizable chunk and would be perfectly willing for
us to use that money to go away. But I don't think that's
fair."

"I see. So you want to sell what's essentially your
family inheritance, your father's books, to even things.
Makes sense. You want to consign me the collection,
you're saying?"

"No, I want to sell it outright, and because you've
always been good to me, forgiven me when I needed
forgiving, I'm willing to let it go extremely reasonably."

He pondered this, poured more wine for each of us from the carafe. "How can I be absolutely sure there aren't some of your old rotten apples buried in the barrel?"

"You can bring over any expert you want to look through them all, one at a time, I don't care. Not that you're not the best expert there is when it comes to a lot of these writers."

"Flattery may get you everywhere but it also makes me nervous. No offense."

"None taken. Not all the books are inscribed, anyway, but most are. A lot of nice association copies."

"Well, no harm in having a look at what we're talking about," he said and asked for the check. "My turn."

I made us some fresh coffee in my apartment and, after calling his assistant to tell her to finish setting up their booth as he was possibly buying some stock, he sat down to look over the books. One by one, I handed them to him, removing and afterward replacing them in their elegant enclosures, explaining who this or that recipient was when he didn't know off the top of his head. Like any seasoned bookman, he carefully placed them in piles based on value, the rarest of them going on a table in an adjacent room for separate appraisal. He seemed satisfied with the authenticity of almost all the works, though cast aside several that seemed suspect or "not right," as he put it. Nor was he wrong in thinking so.

"Anything you don't want, don't take. You have to be happy."

Several long hours transpired before he finally asked, "What kind of money are you thinking?"

I told him I felt that the library was conservatively worth two and a half million retail. More than half a dozen volumes were in the hundred-thousand-dollar range alone, and my 1922 *Ulysses*—the true first, limited to one hundred signed copies, absolutely correct and with its original Aegean-sea-colored blue wrappers in pristine condition, one of my best investments as a collector and a book I truly hated to part with—was worth three hundred easily. That got it to the first million in quick order.

"I want fifty percent of retail," I said. "One and a quarter."

"Well, I appreciate that, but I've got a lot of work ahead of me here to get back to even. What about eight hundred."

Such negotiations were always a dance. We had both done them often enough that the dance felt choreographed much of the time. I knew this was going to be my last dance, the last gesture save one that would ever involve me in books or manuscripts, anything having to do with literary artifacts.

"What about a million and call it done," I said.

"Done," said he, reaching out to shake my hand. He would have to call his bank in the morning to arrange a transfer. "Don't think I have that much sitting in the account, but I can get a short-term loan if need be. They've done it for me before."

"One last thing," I said, resting my palm on the *Ulysses* slipcase as one might on the belly of a sleeping child. "I think it would behoove us not to tell anybody, ever, about this transaction, where you got the books, anything along those lines. My name is mud, some might even say shit, in many circles, as you know. Why needlessly taint such really great books?"

He smiled. "I'm glad you said that, not me. I haven't the least intention of letting on where they came from. A lot of this will be going straight into private collections, anyway. If I didn't have collectors lined up for some of these bigger ticket items, I wouldn't be making the purchase. I hope this helps you. You and Meghan deserve happiness."

It broke my heart to hear him say that. I wanted to tell him I'd changed my mind, it was all a mistake, I wanted to keep the books after all. But I couldn't do that and survive what I knew was a looming threat to my future and freedom. Meghan deserved happiness, yes. But for myself, the abysmal guilt I felt at that moment, a guilt I knew I would carry like a virulent cancer, always growing incrementally, became at one with me and melded with all the other guilt I already wore inside me like festering organs hung on the clothesline of my collarbone. I smiled at him and said, "Thank you."

Meghan was shocked by what I had done without consulting her, although she conceded that I had mentioned the possibility more than once in the past. When I told her the reasoning behind my decision to sell—that I wanted to be a more equal partner in our fledgling marriage—she embraced me, saying we had always been equals and always would be, and for a fleeting moment my guilt was washed away. Besides, I told her, hoping to muddy the waters about the amount of money that had traded hands, I kept a number of mementos from my father's collection. Some, I assured her, were among his favorite volumes of Sherlock Holmes stories for us to pass down the generations.

We did attend the Armory show, which was more crowded than ever. As expected, some booksellers were reserved and polite, others less so, yet others were amicable and congratulated us on the marriage. Curiously, only a few mentioned Adam, expressed their regrets about his death, even though he had been a constant presence here during past fairs. New collectors, I supposed, had simply stepped in to scout the books he once did. Also, it went without saying that given his dabbling in the forger's world, his demise was, to some, good riddance. The farmer does not lament the fox's death. As I inspected book after glorious book, my disciplined gaze always studying the cursive hand and the crude, I was impressed by how few forgeries I encountered. Egotistical as it may sound, I had to wonder if my now-years-ago downfall hadn't scared others away, driven them into some alternative way of eking out a living.

Which brought me to Henry Slader. Not that he hadn't been foremost in my mind from the instant Meghan and I climbed the canopied steps that led up from the sidewalk and entered the Armory. I was sure that somewhere in this cavernous hall, echoing with the voices of intellectuals and investors, buyers and sellers, Slader lurked. My attention was divided, though I did my best to conceal it from Meghan. Whenever I caught anyone looking at me for one single beat longer than seemed natural, I became suspicious, kept an eye on what booth they were in, where they were headed next. I half-expected him to use the comparative safety of the crowd to walk up to me and make a direct confrontation, sotto voce, just two men discussing a transaction, like so many others who were here, elbow to elbow, some in suits, others in jeans—books, not clothes, made the man in this venue—working out deals. But no such confrontation took place. Again I found myself wondering if the threatening letters truly had any meaning and whether my marathon of producing the finest forgeries of my life and selling most of my collection wasn't a fool's errand. If so, I thought, so be it. I felt oddly liberated having done what I did. Liberated from the weight of ownership, yes, and also liberated from the art of forgery, my onetime obsession, because I knew I would never again set pen to paper in that once-erotic, now-exhausted enterprise.

Then I saw him. I didn't know it was him, since how could I? But I knew the face from somewhere. His look oddly combined confidence with furtiveness, disdain with a kind of nervous shyness. His head wasn't shaved but it might as well have been, so tightly shorn was his dark hair to his skull. He was dressed casually, in black like so many other New Yorkers, so far as I could see, though he was several booths away and browsers kept blocking our view of each other. Meghan and I were in the booth of a smart, interesting dealer in photography books, which in recent years had become fashionable and Croesus-expensive to collect. Meg was very much in her element here, given her interest in visual art folios. I told her I'd be back in a minute and she said "great" without looking up from a Walker Evans volume that enthralled her.

Nervous as I had ever been but knowing I had his blood money, I threaded my way past fairgoers in his direction. Rather than approaching me, as I had expected, he melted into the crowd. I stood where I was and peered ahead, looking for that face to reappear. Where had I seen him before?

Soon enough there he was again, farther away this time, closer to the exit, looking over his shoulder at me but not signaling me to follow, standing there like a lurid apparition. It was then I recognized who he was. Of course, I thought. Last year at Adam's graveside service. The plainclothes cop. The man I'd assumed was there in search of a murderer compelled to visit if not the scene of his crime then some proximate scene that might make his crime feel less abstract, more real.

Slader must have read my thoughts at that moment, because his pale face slowly broke into a faint smile. He tipped his chin down and then snapped it back up. Yes, this is me, his gestures meant. Rather than turn on my heel and walk away, rather than remain stock still, as physically frozen as I was mentally, I nodded in acknowledgment. But acknowledgment of what? Was I conceding I had murdered Adam Diehl when in fact Slader himself had more reason to commit such an act than I ever did? Look at him. Even if he didn't have the stock face of a killer, a visage bleak and ruthless and with an old knife scar on his cheek, say, he did look determined, single-minded, a taker. My fear of the man mutated into a feeling more akin to anger, even hatred. Who did he think he was? It seemed reasonable that I ought to walk right past him, ignoring anything he might say to me, and speak to the uniformed guard who stood by the exit, tell him there was a murderer in the building, finger Henry Slader then and there, and let the chips fall where they may. The wall that stood between me and that rash action was my newfound happiness with Meghan, my marriage and the dream of a life together away from here, from all the sorrows and strife we had known. Too, if Slader was arrested, my

fresh sale of counterfeits would doubtless be discovered, since he would sing the same accusatory song as I
did and turn rigorous scrunity right back at me, landing
me, no doubt, behind bars again. This time for a very
long stretch and with no Meghan to greet me when I
was finally released. As I saw it, there was one sole path
for me to get out of this predicament. A scree-strewn,
hazardous path with a guide I loathed but was bound
to follow.

I looked down, up, and he was gone. Realizing
Meghan must be wondering where I was—though she
was altogether aware that I tended to wander off and
lose myself at these fairs—I made my way down the
crowded corridor toward where Slader had stood, looking for him in the milling throng and, seeing him nowhere, returned to the photography booth. Not finding
my wife there, I panicked. Had Slader doubled back to
speak with her directly while I stood mesmerized in
an aisle nearer the exit? As a child I got lost only once,
having wandered away from my mother in a depart-
ment store, and the same wretched feelings of terror
and abandonment that seized me then did so now. In a
sweat, I now found myself searching out two people, one
loved, the other hated. Five relentless minutes passed as
I made my way around the fair in a sweat, bumping
into people and muttering apologies like some fool, not
knowing what I would do if I encountered Slader and
Meghan together.

"There you are," Meghan said, her hand laid on my
shoulder from behind. "Are you all right?"

"I'm fine, no worries," I managed.

"You sure? You look like you saw a ghost."

"Well, neither a ghost nor any books I can't live with-out," I said, skating past her comment as best I could. "What about you, anything you can't live without?"

"Other than yourself, nothing," she said.

With that we left the Armory. No further sighting of my accuser, my extortionist. As we strolled back downtown along stately Park Avenue and scruffy lower Broadway, the faltering promise of freedom, if only I could square things away with Slader, seemed at once near and far. I knew that, just as one cannot force a flower to blossom by pulling on its petals, I had to be patient, bide my time, and hold out hope that my frag-ile dream would come to pass.

KENMARE IT WAS. The village where we got engaged, the magical locus where we felt the happiest. We let a small cottage, not far from the lodge where we had stayed, on a vigorous creek punctuated by muscular bantam waterfalls and populated by salmon and trout that flashed in the morning light when they leapt. Although English was spoken here in the southern part of the country, as in most every part of Ireland except for little pockets known as Gaeltacht areas, we studied Gaelic together, a language that more than rivaled German for its crazy polysyllabics and unpronounceable pile-ups of consonants, and made day trips to Dingle to converse with locals. We made a few friends, not many, but all of them good-hearted folk who had grown up in County Kerry and wisely never left. We hiked MacGillycuddy's Reeks; we loved taking the ferry out to the Skellig isles where monks once lived in utter austerity, cut off from the outside world like the pillar saints of old, atop their barren rocks hundreds of feet above the gnawing ocean. Our days were filled with simple tasks—sweeping the kitchen, shopping at the market for dinner, reading and writing, breathing, being.

One midsummer day we shared a paper bag lunch of black bread, olives, and local cheeses at one of our favorite places in all of Kenmare, an impressive neolithic stone circle known as the Shrubberies, a few minutes' walk from the center of town. Despite being near the somewhat busy Cromwell's Bridge and a stone's throw from the village's main streets, this ancient circle—egg-shaped, actually—of fifteen boulders, a baker's dozen of them upright, centered by an impressive boulder burial, was utterly quiet. Birdsong, occasional respectful visitors speaking in low tones, the distant, whisper-soft white noise of unseen traffic, these were all that disturbed the otherwise sanctum-sanctorum hush of the place. In our self-taught crash course to learn as much about our adopted home as we could, Meghan and I discovered that the Irish name for Kenmare was An Neidín, which meant "the Little Nest." Perfect, we thought, even before we came upon the Shrubberies which, to us, was a nest within a nest.

Sitting alone on one of the sun-warmed boulders that had been placed there thousands of years before, feeling a little sacrilegious given it was a burial site, we said nothing for a time. It was curious, our silence in this silent place, as Meghan and I were usually involved in a constantly streaming dialogue. Without either of us saying as much, we each knew what the other was thinking. Maybe we had managed to break the bonds that held

us back in the States, break away from our different orphan stories to forge a new life together. Sure, Meghan
had lost her parents in a single tragic event while mine
had died separately, one slowly eaten alive by cancer,
the other felled by a heart attack. And whereas I never
had a sibling to turn to, hers—one whose very lifeblood
derived from her, it seemed—was gone. We were both
alone and anything but alone. I looked at her, then
glanced away toward the enclosure of pristine fir trees,
thinking, Yes, we'll make this work, a pair of orphans
together forging a new life.

What ever happened to the word "forge" that it
had acquired such an ugly meaning, I wondered, my
thoughts straying. Here was a term that indicated slow
and steady progress, a forging ahead against odds. A
forge was a hearth, a furnace in whose fiery heat the
blacksmith pounded metal into the useful shapes of
horseshoes, andirons, tools with which to build. Way
back in the fourteenth century, at a time when different
people gathered at this stone circle, to forge meant to
create, to make and shape, like a Joycean smithy of the
soul. When did the virtue go out of this beautiful old
word? When did it evolve into a derogatory that meant
to defraud, to counterfeit, to falsify? And yet who was
I to think such thoughts in this place as old as Stone-
henge, older than the dirty definition of forgery, I who
embodied the definition of the evil side of this otherwise noble word?

As I had no answer to this last question, it was one
I recognized I needed to let go of that day and hope it
never returned.

Yes, Slader did contact me again. This time his letter
stipulated a place and time for us to meet. I suppose that

given we had encountered and recognized one another at the fair, the ice was broken, as it were, and getting together to cut our deal was somehow less an onerous, appalling task. Prior to our meeting, I got it in my head to make one last beautiful forgery before depositing what was left of my pens, my inks, and other paraphernalia in the garbage. I bested Slader's Baskerville archive, writing it out verbatim, not unlike Pierre Menard with his *Don Quixote* in Borges's story, correcting any and all minute flaws in the calligraphy, getting Doyle's sometimes idiosyncratic hand just right. During our minute-long exchange in a Greek coffee shop not far from Washington Square—the James allusion couched in the rendezvous spot Slader named was not lost on me—I gave him back his "original" knowing that a newer original now existed, far closer to what the master would have scribed, had he ever done so in the first place.

"We're done?" I asked him.

I noticed he seemed far more nervous than I felt.

"Because we had better be done," I ventured, trying to set on my face a steely look of both resolve and threat. I didn't envy him his messy life, a life entangled in profit and deceit, secrecy and inevitable ruin. Myself, I was finished with all that, or so I hoped with an almost religious fervency, a fervency that quite nearly equaled the passion that used to be reserved for the intimate acts of forgery in which I used to luxuriate.

"Done," he said and, without counting the money or peering inside the manila envelope that housed his Baskerville forgery, left. Out of nowhere, one of my favorite lines in all of Conan Doyle's Holmes adventures came to mind as I watched him disappear out the door, a line in "The Adventure of the Blue Carbuncle," in which Holmes introduces himself to the hapless, rat-faced larcenist at the center of that mystery. This man—a white-cheeked, would-be jewel thief named James Ryder—responds to Holmes's statement, "I think that I could be of assistance to you," by demanding, "You? Who are you? How could you know anything of the matter?" Holmes tells the naif his name and then defines his entire purpose in life, his philosophy and fundamental creed. "It is my business," he says, "to know what other people don't know." Words to live by, I thought when I first read that sentence in my very early teens. Words to live by.

Meghan sold a large percentage of her bookshop to a collective of her employees with very generous terms for payment. Indeed, we dispossessed ourselves of almost everything aside from clothing, a few favorite books, various childhood souvenirs. My car went to a junkyard where the scrappers gave me a hundred dollars, which happened to be more than the thing was worth on the market. As a personal gesture to Atticus Moore, one meant silently to atone for having sold him those forgeries, I consigned most of what was left of my permanent collection, telling him to send me whatever he thought was fair for what he realized in sales whenever it was convenient, and no rush about it. No, this didn't erase my treachery but it somehow drew off, at least to my mind, a little of its poison. These monies plus the proceeds from the Montauk sale gave us a comfortable cushion and the freedom to start over as we saw fit.

Meghan and I drove one day to our favorite restaurant in Kinsale, a seafood joint called Fishy Fishy, where just-caught hake and haddock were served in the cool blue shade of awnings outdoors. We were trading the

small talk of contented married folks against the background of seagulls screeching and chattering over the
bay when she said something that caught me off guard.

"I have a question I've been wanting to ask for the
longest time." She spoke in a tone of voice that was perfectly even, betraying not an iota of accusation or even
particular concern.

"What's that, darling woman."

"It's a stupid question and you'll probably laugh at
me—"

"Nothing you say is stupid," I assured her, taking a
sip from my pint of Beamish.

"You never visited my brother out in Montauk before we were together, did you?"

"No, like I've always said, we really only knew each
other at fairs and in the occasional bookshop."

"And you and I never went out there once we started
seeing each other."

Where was she going with this, I wondered, and
waited, shaking my head.

"So how was it you knew the way to the bungalow
that first morning when you drove us out there? No
map and no directions from me?"

Taken aback, I couldn't afford to pause a moment
longer than I did before saying, "But you're wrong.
You're not remembering right. You did give directions."

Her turn to hesitate. "You're sure about that?"

Encouraged by her uncertainty, I insisted it was impossible I could ever have found my way to his ocean-
side door on my own. Persuaded, she tucked her hair
behind her ear and offered me one of her smiles so
richly touched by love that I felt there were few men
alive more fortunate than I.

JUST AS A STORM can abruptly replace a sunny Kenmare day with gale-driven rain that renders umbrellas useless and gives Ireland its reputation for capricious rotten weather, my feelings of peace were punctuated by moments of sudden dread. Now and again, an out-of-the-blue fear of the mailman reminded me of the bad old days. If I caught a stranger on the street eyeing me with what I considered unseemly curiosity, a bolt of familiar panic would seize my viscera and make my hands go icy cold. Even when I heard the rare burst of local police car sirens, however different they sounded from the wailing music of their counterparts in the States, a sour taste rose into my mouth, the acid taste of guilt I suppose one might say.

And yet most of the time I found relief in forgetfulness about my past. An ocean did, after all, separate

me from my former life. Whatever bad things I had or
hadn't done were behind me now, so I reassured myself.
At night, in our warm bed, while listening to Meghan
softly breathing in her sleep and watching the constellations wheel with magisterial slowness and godly
indifference across the black sky outside our window,
I reasoned there was no further need to worry about
anything. A year and a half had clocked by since Adam's
death, and the murder case was as cold as the black
interstices between the stars above. Atticus Moore, true
to his word, sent along the occasional check for my
share in the books I had consigned him, always with a
brief and upbeat note that never once suggested he'd
run into any problems with the works I had forged.
Slader had, it seemed, disappeared back into the rotten
woodwork from whence he came.

Taking advantage of Meghan's birthright, we had
filed our papers and were able to take part-time jobs,
as much to get ourselves more involved in our adopted
community as to earn any wage. Meghan clerked in the
local bookstore, well stocked with Irish history and lit-
erature, maps, and, yes, art- and cookbooks. Myself, I
found work in a stationer's that had a nifty letterpress
printing shop in the back, complete with a Vandercook proof press I was eager to learn to operate. Each
of us was in our element. With this litany of reassur-
ances, I would shut my eyes and drift into a dreamless
sleep. Looking back on this calm period in my life, I
wonder if dreams during sleep were unnecessary. I was
already living a dream every waking hour, despite the
occasional dark cloud of fear that came over me, the
understandable fear this all might be somehow taken
away.

News that would forever change my life, news that was every bit as unexpected as receiving a Henry James letter in the mail or a policeman's knock on the door but that carried none of their calamitous misfortune, came on a nondescript Sunday morning several months into our Kenmare sojourn.

Meghan and I, inveterate early risers, always slept in late on Sundays. We tried never to make plans that would involve anything other than a nice, lazy start to the day. Scrambled eggs and blanched cherry tomatoes, rashers, some black and white puddings, fresh coffee, the newspaper—this was our idea of perfection. So I was taken aback when I awoke on the second Sunday in August to find that my wife had gone downstairs and started what was to be a surprise breakfast. Wasn't my birthday. Wasn't any day I could remember as being special. Drawn by the smell of ground espresso beans, I put on my robe and went down to join her.

"What's up?" I asked. "We win the lottery?"

"Here," she said, and handed me a glass of orange juice.

"Well, did we?" taking a sip.

"You might say we did," was her response. "Sit. Let's eat."

Though I was keen to know what was going on, I played along and asked no further questions. We were halfway into our breakfast when Meghan set her fork on her plate and said, without any prefatory comment, "I'm pregnant."

Beside those words and the look on the face of the woman who uttered them, I had neither heard nor seen anything more moving in my life. Without a sound I got up out of my chair, rounded the breakfast table, and took Meghan into my arms. After all the heartache she had suffered and courage she'd shown, it was as if a sluice gate inside her had opened, allowing a flood of tears to come forth. I kissed her moist eyes, held her close, told her we would do everything in our power to make this the happiest, healthiest, wisest, most coddled baby ever. I couldn't remember being so lighthearted, so rapturous, even during the bygone times when the act of forgery produced similar feelings.

The rest of the day swung back and forth from unfettered giddiness to a more mature conversation about whether we needed to find new lodgings, if we were absolutely certain we wanted to raise our boy or girl in rural Ireland rather than New York, how long Meghan would continue to work at the bookshop, and so forth. Despite our dizzy glee over the prospect of raising a child together and probably not being in the proper state of mind to make rational decisions, most of what we settled on would prove to be the way we later agreed things should go. There was plenty of room in the furnished cottage we'd leased. Besides, we liked it here. The grove of soughing pines that edged the field behind the house, the dancing creek nearby, the house itself with its thatched roof and cozy fireplaces—what child wouldn't want to grow up in such an idyllic environment as this? Manhattan wasn't a place that drew us much at all anymore and, unbeknown to my wife, of course, it wasn't a place I might ever like to set foot in again, if I had my druthers.

"Can I put in a couple of name requests early?" Meghan asked that afternoon as we walked arm in arm after taking a drive over to Bantry Bay to watch the rollers come in and the fishing boats bob like carved and painted corks atop the heavy swells.

"You bet," I said.

"Well, okay. If it's a girl I want to name her after your mother, Nicole."

"She'd have been very honored. And if it's a boy?"

"If it's a boy, and you don't have any objections, I'd love to name him Adam."

I could easily come up with any number of objections to naming our son Adam, not the least of which would be, Why drape the albatross of a murdered man's name over the shoulders of our son? Instead, I simply said, "That sounds fine, great. I thought you were going to say William Butler."

"Well, it could be Adam William Butler, or William Butler Adam, you know."

"Fortunately, we have months to settle on names. Right now, I couldn't even tell you my own name. I love you, Meghan."

"And I love you."

The rest of August floated by without incident as summer gave way to early fall, and the throngs of tourists—Americans, Japanese, Germans—passing through on their way to visiting the Ring of Kerry were now thinning. Then, no warning, it was as if my life simply collapsed in on itself like a sheet of paper wadded into a ball. Walking home after an evening pint in my favorite pub in the village, far up at the top of the street, I could swear I saw Henry Slader looking me right in the eye before ducking around the corner. Rather than reverse course to take an alternate route home, I found myself half-running up the block, pushing my way past other pedestrians, cursing under my breath. Those nights of lying awake, mentally parading through a host of ways my current Eden could witness a second fall had, it seemed, not been altogether a fool's game.

Naturally, ridiculously, when I made it to the corner he was nowhere to be seen. It reminded me of that awful moment in the Armory when I glanced down for a moment and he vanished before I looked back up. Yet he wasn't some ghostly magician or supernatural revenant. Quite the opposite, Slader had proven himself to be very much of this world, a man capable of all manner of very ugly, very human desires and faults. Hadn't he said we were done when I handed over, to the last dollar, the money he demanded and his now-second-rate cache of fake Conan Doyle letters? Didn't the man have anything better to do than harass me, someone who had treated him fairly, honored my end of the bargain?

Like a puppet on a string, I marched along the sidewalk that paralleled the main road, moving quickly in the direction I thought I had seen him headed. After a minute of frenzied searching, I stopped to catch my wheezing breath—it seemed I had developed a mild case of asthma since moving to this rainy clime. As I stood there, homeward-bound cars coasting along the roadway and some of the same people I had jostled past now overtaking me, I began seriously to doubt myself. If it had in fact been Slader, he wouldn't have bothered to run away from me, would he? What would be the purpose of such evasion at this point in our, granted, bizarre and unsavory acquaintance? An uneasy sense of calm came over me as I reasoned with myself, breath slowing, that there are more doppelgängers running around out there than any of us dare imagine. This was not my Henry Slader, not here in faraway County Kerry, in a little village tucked away down near the bottom of the isle of Eire. It was, instead, pure paranoia.

Determined not to let this hallucination overcome the calm my life had settled into, I returned to the cozy comfort of the pub, called Meghan at work, and asked her if she'd like to come along and join me for some mutton stew, maybe a bit of trad music. Just because we were married and pregnant didn't mean we couldn't have some good distracting fun. My nerves needed another pint or two, although of course I didn't dare tell her why. She was delighted at the idea, and once the bookstore closed—it stayed open an hour later than the stationery shop—she came straight over and we had a fine night of it. Despite the age-old "Guinness is good for you" myth that suggested even pregnant women in need of health-giving iron benefited from drinking stout, Meghan refrained. But her high spirits belied her sobriety. She laughed and clapped and sang along with some of the songs she knew. Myself, I deliberately pushed my preposterous Slader lookalike out of mind and listened to the singers play guitar and tin whistle, fiddle and bodhrán for a couple of hours. For all the glow I got on, I reminded myself I was an expectant father now. The kind of man I would want raising my child was not one who would glance at faces around the room with a bugbear foreboding. Rather, it would be my job to explain away hobgoblins, gremlins, ogres, and all the other assorted harmless monsters that hide under beds—not to be living in fear of them myself. If my years as a forger were truly behind me, as now they had to be since I was no longer an adult child who felt it was all right to do whatever I pleased and damn all, I knew I must change. Change now, change categorically, change for good.

Our bill settled, we left the pub to find a misty, starless night outside that was not at all cold. The colorful lights of other pubs up and down the main block were reflected in pools of rainwater on the narrow street.

"Shall we walk home?" she asked.

"And leave the car where it's parked?"

"Sure, why not? It'll be safe, no problem. I locked it."

"Well, walking's what I originally intended."

"So you said. No reason not to follow through. We can leave a little early and walk back in the morn."

The house was not quite two kilometers from the center of Kenmare village and our stroll home was quiet, with Meghan humming one of the songs we had heard. My Slader sighting aside, calmed by the pub fare and tired from the walk, I slept like the dead that night and woke up predawn next morning full of vigor. We had already chosen the bedroom adjacent to ours as the nursery and were repainting it a cheery yellow— no pink or blue for us, as we decided we didn't want to know the baby's gender until it was born. Seeing I had an extra hour on my hands, I rolled out a second coat of acrylic on one of the walls by a window that overlooked a spacious span of mowed field behind the cottage. As the sun rose, the grass that extended to the curtain of mature slouch-boughed pines at the end of our yard changed from dark forest green to the bright emerald unique to this landscape—the very shade of emerald green used by William Morris and other Victorians in their wallpapers, which was mixed with arsenic and produced lethal fumes. Death by William Morris wallpaper, who would have thought it possible? Oh, the trivia a good forger must know, I thought, as the dew winked and twinkled in the lawn, making it look as if diamonds had been scattered there by some beneficent creature of the night.

As I painted, I glanced now and then out the window, imagining how many mornings our boy or girl would view this same sylvan scape with wonder—that is, once he or she was tall enough to peer on tiptoes past the sill. It reminded me of my own childhood weekend home in upstate New York, where my parents retreated with almost fanatical regularity from Friday nights through Sunday evenings, to escape the city and, as my father put it, "recharge the batteries." Didn't matter what case he was involved with or whether he had to make business calls and prepare rebuttals or cross-examinations, pore over testimony, whatever his practice demanded. He always did it in an office attached to our restored farmhouse in the Hudson Valley. So it was that I as a youth had a view out my window that wasn't altogether unlike this one. Grass and more grass, a valance of flowers in summer, and at the periphery a tall partition of trees beyond which lay a forest.

This visual memory was as strong as any from my past and prompted the question, What kind of father was I going to be? My own dad, looking back, wasn't unassailable, but he presented a model to aspire to, perhaps one that was both too good to be true and thus undesirable because unattainable. Who knows. But as for me? I had much to hide and knew I would always be looking out at the forest edge with different eyes than I did in my youth. I who had never been afraid of what might lurk in the dark woods now couldn't feel quite so self-assured as before, would have to consider the slim but real possibility the forest was looking back at me, framed here in the window.

Dying is, once again, a dangerous business, but so is living. In fatherhood I would have to find a new fearlessness and at the same time be protective of my too-vulnerable family. I realized in that moment how much easier it had been to avoid, erase, ignore such thoughts before Meghan discovered she was pregnant. Now this exile of sorts was no longer a perfect displacement from life and lives past. I would just have to deal with it, and the best way, it seemed as I rolled some fresh paint along the dado, was to embrace anew the fact—and it was a fact, damned if it wasn't—that I was a free man with not a single consequential finger pointed in my direction.

Meghan had entered the room silent as fog. "You plan on going to work today, Picasso?"

"Oh man, you startled me," I rasped, wheeling around.

"I'm sorry, didn't mean to," said Meghan, a bit startled herself. "We've got to get going soon though, since we have to walk, remember?"

It was true, I had utterly forgotten we left the car in town. Hurriedly cleaning things up, I changed into my casual work clothes, and we set off.

"That was kind of strange," she said, after we turned out of the drive and headed down the dirt lane toward the paved road that led to the village. "I never saw you lock the door before."

"I hadn't even realized I did."

"You all right, Will?"

The answer was clearly no, but I assured her, "Fine, I'm fine," startled at hearing my name, a name I never

much liked. Usually endearments—none of which need
be listed here, as we are all guilty of the same maudlin
sobriquets—dislodged my given name from our conversation, which was fine by me. Shadow men never like
being called by name, I guess one could say, although
now that I was out of the shadows, why shouldn't I
shout my name from mountaintops? Habit, caution,
self-disgust? I was definitely off this morning and didn't
like it. "It's just that I was thinking how isolated the
house is. Hope the little one won't be scared of the
dark."

Meghan gave a relieved laugh and told me I was
getting way ahead of myself. "Besides," she said, taking
my hand as we strolled along beside the hedgerow, "it's
good to be scared of the dark sometimes."

IN LOCKING DOORS—of cottages, cars, any other thing with a key and bolt—we reveal what we treasure. What we desire to protect from others, be they prying or covetous. I thought about Meghan's offhand yet inarguable comment the rest of that morning. What I most needed to protect had no fail-safe lock or key. Nor was it something I treasured. Rather, I wondered, was it an act that had by now become so unreal to me as not to exist? Fortunately business was brisk at work, and anxieties about our cottage or car—the latter was unmolested, of course—dispersed as the day wore on.

As it turned out, to my joyful chagrin, Henry Slader was also so unreal as not to exist. At least, not in Kenmare. I spotted the bastard again during my lunch hour, this time as he climbed out of a parked car, helped an elderly woman from the passenger side, and escorted her into a pharmacy. The resemblance was uncanny, and as I followed him inside I recognized a familiar stature, even a familiar face, but when I heard him speak in a distinctly Irish brogue, relief came over me the likes of which no drug on any shelf at any dosage in the place could possibly have afforded me. I was never more delighted to feel like a perfect imbecile.

That said, I did stop by the hardware store after work to make an enquiry about who in Kenmare might be hired to install security lights at the cottage. Assuming Meghan would agree with my idea, I decided to propose to our landlord that we would let him approve the lighting design and that, in turn, we would pay for everything, including whatever increase there might be in the utility bill. Yes, I realized one of the many reasons we settled in pretty Kenmare was that crime was so low. This was, as far as we could tell, misdemeanor country at worst. Petty theft or, say, the occasional reveler who'd overindulged and maybe broken a window or a nose in schnockered exuberance because his favorite hurling team had won their match, his favorite footballer had scored the winning goal. Still, I knew myself well enough to know my concerns about security at the cottage had taken root, foolish or otherwise, and rather than let them fester it was better to take action. What was more, it occurred to me that when I explained to Mr. Sullivan, whose family had owned the house for generations, that we had lost Meghan's brother to a violent crime in the hours between midnight and predawn, he would be understanding in the extreme. Indeed, how could he not agree? It would constitute a free improvement to his property.

While Mr. Sullivan did like and approve the project —he generously offered to pay half the costs, as it happened—Meghan was less sure.

"Don't get me wrong," she said, over lunch in town a few days later, after having met with the contractor. "It does get dark there at night, especially when there's no moon or the sky's clouded over—"

"Which is often enough."

"Which is often enough. But I'm just concerned you're overworrying the whole thing. Locking the doors, which I might add we rarely did for the first months, really ought to suffice. It's not like this is New York, you know."

I scratched my cheek and looked past her for a moment before agreeing, "Well, no, it's not. I suppose it's normal to want to protect my family, now that we're really going to be a family. But if you don't think it's necessary we don't have to move ahead with it."

Her turn to think. She reached across the table and rested her hand on mine, in a gentle, almost mothering way. "You do what you think's best."

"We can play croquet by halogen floodlight," I said, trying for a little joke, relieved the discussion was over and that Meghan was, while not foursquare behind me, at least tolerant of my idea. Whether I was being paranoid after my false Slader sighting, which did stir up some old but logical fears, was beside the point, I assured myself as I asked our waiter for the bill.

What Meghan said next surprised me so much I didn't know how to respond. "You know, I owe you an apology."

"About this lighting stuff? No apologies and no worries."

"No, I mean, listen. Sometimes it's too easy for me to forget that Adam's murder had a huge impact on your life, too. He was my brother and we were very close, maybe even too close. He really depended a lot on me. Probably needed more from me than I was able to give him, especially after I met you."

I felt my feet freeze, as if they had been abruptly encased in ice blocks. "No, Meghan, don't worry," I started to say.

"But when he died in such an awful way, I know I probably was harsh with you. I remember some of what I said, and it wasn't always very kind. So I want to apologize for that. What I'm trying to say here is, I get it with the door locking and these security lights and your concerns about the cottage being rural and all of it. If Adam had locked his doors, had motion sensor lights for instance, who knows?"

"Meghan—"

"I need to honor your loss, since you lost Adam, too," and with that she gently wept.

We left the restaurant, our arms around each other as if supporting wounded comrades staggering off a battlefield. What could I say? Many crosscurrenting thoughts flew about in my head but the one that made most sense was to say nothing. So I remained mute as I walked her back to the bookstore, dropped her off after she daubed her eyes with my scarf, and returned to the contractor's office to sign papers.

"How soon can we get started?" I asked.

"Beginning of next week," he said.

"And while we're at it, I'm wondering if you wouldn't mind giving me an estimate for an alarm system. You know, doors and downstairs windows."

I took off the following week from work in order to oversee the job or, that is, watch the installation from a close distance. Doing my best not to be underfoot as the electricians began wiring lights beneath the thatched eaves, I spent much of my time in the nursery-to-be, where I completed the walls and trim, then started refinishing the bassinet Meghan and I had bought in an antique shop up in Killarney. The building was old, obviously, and getting the alarm contacts in place and functional demanded at times a bit of ingenuity, as did digging narrow trenches in the rocky yard to bury electric cable for several peripheral ground lights positioned near the forest edges. But the men were experienced and work went smoothly. When the undertaking was finished, Meghan brought home a celebratory bottle of cider and only half-jokingly toasted, "Here's to a thousand and one nights of unworried sleep." We walked the perimeter of the yard after nightfall, taking our glasses with us, as the lights illuminated not just the house but the surrounding field, sending long shadows out behind individual trees that stood here and there in the yard. It was quite a sight, exactly what I had hoped for. Night could instantly become day if I ever heard an unusual, disturbing sound outdoors after we'd retired. While Meghan had every right to deem this security project of mine the unnecessary act of an already overprotective father, at the end of the day she was happy to see me happy. "You could be spending our hard-earned money on worse things," she added.

Fact was, I still found myself looking over my shoulder for no apparent reason, and as for my sleep, it remained dreamless but continued to be troubled by bouts of insomnia. I knew the hours when constellations would rise into view and the moon, traveling endlessly through its phases, would appear to shed a soft eddying light across our bedroom. I reasoned with myself that we had found as safe an asylum as could be hoped for and chided myself for becoming a seek-sorrow, one who can find trouble and torment even where there is none.

The very next week, news that the police—or, that is, the one detective who continued to be interested in Adam Diehl's cold case, the guy who had turned up that chilly day at the funeral—had brought a man in for further questioning stirred up a whole host of emotions. Our fragile calm was fractured, with hope lifting my wife's spirits and covert panic dampening mine.

Meghan got the call from Montauk on the day Henry Slader was let go a second time in not quite as many years for lack of evidence. The officer, whose name was Pollock, like the painter, told her he just wanted her to know about the interrogation and that he was still following any leads, going over old evidence, trying to keep the search for her brother's murderer alive, so to say. At my insistence she told me, twice from beginning to end, everything that the detective had related. It was all I could do not to request that she walk through the conversation word for word yet a third time. As it stood, I probably betrayed far more interest in Pollock and Slader's meeting than was necessary or, for that matter, prudent. And yet Meghan's unnerving apology to me for her failure to acknowledge the impact of Adam's death on my own life provided a good justification for my hypercuriosity about this call. My keen interest in the news about Slader could reasonably be attributed to concern about justice for Adam. So, I believed, it must have seemed to my wife, and that was for the best. The truth was I felt a raw and desperate unease about Slader and Slader alone.

"What's the next move?" I asked, figuring I would soon have to let it go, lest it look to her like another obsession along the same lines as the outdoor security lights and alarm system—which indeed it was. "Did he say what happens now?"

"Not really, just that he intends to keep at it."

"He sounds more hopeful they'll catch somebody? Seems pretty devoted to the case."

She pulled her hair back with both hands and frowned, an anything-but-hopeful look in her eyes. "He told me again that he'd give his eyetooth if he could go back in time and be there to direct the first responders who contaminated the crime scene. One was a rookie and the other a seasonal, is what he said. And forensics, for all the movies and miniseries that portray it as miracle work, is a science that depends on clean evidence."

Guilt is unbecoming in the guilty. That is what I thought, listening to the last of Meghan's narrative of her overseas phone call. After overcoming the initial surprise at hearing that my nemesis had been dragged from whatever lair he'd been operating out of—was he still making forgeries?—I found myself looking at the bright side. Or not so much looking at it as basking in the odd glow of a fact that hadn't initially occurred to me. And that was this. If the authorities were at such an impasse that they had nothing better to do than interrogate old Slader again, Slader who was guilty of nothing more than fraud, extortion, avarice, and who knows what other pedestrian misdeeds, it meant they had no viable case against a living soul. And, in particular, against me.

For an uncanny, fleeting moment it dawned on me that I myself had somehow managed to become my own best forgery. Were it not for my authentic love for Meghan and the expectant love a father-to-be feels for his unborn child, love that for better or worse does tether one to some trace of morality—a word as suspect as *permanence* and *reality*—I would be ready to take my place in the pantheon of forgers, most all of whom were prime examples of life imitating their art. But I wasn't there yet. One expert remained at large who could yet attempt to declare me, like a cache of magnificently faked Sherlock Holmes letters, to be not what I seemed. While I told Meghan how great it was that Pollock was still on the case, what silently concerned and even annoyed me most about his hapless efforts was that they might have awakened a beast best left asleep.

WHEREAS I ADMIRED MY FATHER, I adored my mother. My father's legacy as a book collector was key to my education about literary first editions, and the debt I owe to him about all things Arthur Conan Doyle, indeed all things rare books, could never be overstated. But it was my mother—several of whose watercolors were hung in our Kenmare cottage, charming landscapes that reminded Meghan a little of those by W. B. Yeats's brother, Jack—whose influence on me was of paramount importance when it came to calligraphic prowess.

The illustrated nursery rhyme and fairy tale books Meghan and I had begun to collect into a little library for our child were, in my youth, read to me by my mother as I sat on her lap and marveled at the colorful pictures of princes and princesses, runaway bunnies

and velveteen rabbits, wild things and talking animals, all
manner of other fanciful characters. When, in elemen-
tary school, my teachers urged me to write with my right
hand, it was my mother who intervened on my behalf,
telephoning the principal to demand that they allow
me to follow my natural southpaw instincts. My mom,
champion of nonconformity and a lefty herself, won the
day and henceforth I became the lefthander that genet-
ics demanded, a minor challenge to my later work as a
forger though obviously one over which I triumphed.
Once I was a precocious six or seven, it was my mom
who took me to the Frick, the Morgan, the Met, and
showed me not only old master paintings and Roman
frescoes but the astonishing paintings William Blake
made to surround his poems, the meanings of which she
patiently tried to explain to me. It was my wonderful
mom who, seeing my youthful interest in calligraphy,
made sure that I saw master Japanese scrollwork from
this or that dynasty at the Asia Society and a major ex-
hibit of illuminated medieval manuscripts at the New
York Public Library. And it was my mom who sat me
down with ink and paints, brushes and nibbed pens, and
taught me how to approach the glorious tabula rasa of
a blank sheet of paper. She who first showed me how to
copy written characters and words on tracing paper and
later, after setting aside any such nets to catch my figura-
tive falls, how to see the finished line before that line is
even drawn on a beautiful piece of handmade foolscap.

My mother saw to it that every impediment to an
early mastery of the calligraphic arts was removed from
my path. Any true portrait of the artist as a young forger
would have to include her as my teacher, my prompter,
my consoler, with the obvious proviso that never in a

million years would she have wanted me to become what I became. She was a mentor, not a prophetess. As a mother, she gave her boy tools with which to build secular cathedrals, not elegant outhouses, as she would surely have viewed the forger's enterprise. That I preferred outhouses, to continue the metaphor, was never her hope nor her fault. I found my way to that proclivity all on my very own.

I remember my first lessons from her as she encouraged me to try my hand at forming letters in chancery cursive script while sitting next to her at the kitchen table of our upstate farmhouse. As always, I began by doing doodle exercises to warm up, drawing parallel S-curves that resembled abstract waves or thick straight verticals that looked like a bamboo fence or, and this was perhaps what astonished her most, forming perfect circle after perfect concentric circle. But doodles weren't chancery cursive any more than a classic stick figure is a da Vinci pastel nude. At first I found the whole business foreign and frustrating. But I liked being near her—I was admittedly something of an asocial fellow at school, prone to either sulk through classes or get myself into physical altercations that resulted in suspensions—and so I persisted. Whenever the principal barred me from class for days or weeks after I'd found myself in a fistfight, I far preferred the tutoring I got at home to anything I learned formally in the school system. Without ever admitting it to the authorities, my parents, or even to myself at the time, my motivation for getting into trouble had less to do with striking back at a bully or roughing up some kid who rubbed me the wrong way than that it afforded me a chance to spend more time with my mom.

I must have been around twelve years old when I surpassed her in technical skill. I could replicate most every writing style reproduced in her calligraphy manuals and history books—oh, there were some hoary scrawls such as the earliest Magna Carta, scribbled with iron gall ink on parchment, that I had no interest in bothering with—matching word for word what was on the page and signing my own name in all manner of various hands. Rather than compete, though, she only urged me on.

When she was diagnosed with thyroid cancer, she put a brave face on it and continued to work with me as long as she was physically able. Having run out of handwriting samples for me to copy, we turned to my father's collection for inspiration. In retrospect, she must have been fully aware he would disapprove but went ahead with our exercises anyway. We kept it secret from him that I soon excelled in copying out respectable facsimiles of some of his Conan Doyle letters and manuscripts. Did the potential ethical issues that might surround our then-innocent activities disturb her? I have no idea, but doubt it. These were not forgeries I was producing, after all, because I wasn't even attempting to replicate the paper or even the exact color of ink the master had used, nor did either of us ever consider defrauding someone by offering them for sale as originals. No, it was just the size, shape, form, and figure of the words that interested me. Obsessed me, really. And made her proud. When I finished copying a warm personal epistle to one of the author's friends, for instance, a part of my soul merged with Doyle's, or so I fancied in my greenhorn naivete.

When my dear mother Nicole died at thirty-six—
seven long years younger than I myself am now—my
father's response was, at least to my teenage mind, in-
conceivable and frightening. Rather than mourning her
as I did, instead of crying or seeming to miss her at all,
he charged forward with his lawyering and bought, as
far as I could tell, more expensive books than ever before. My admiration remained strong. He was all I had.
But he confused me nonetheless. Looking back, he was
obviously suffering greatly. His brother, a civil engineer,
and sister, a homemaker, as women used to be called
who worked impossibly hard to keep a household and
family running, were neither of them very close to him.
Indeed, after they dutifully attended the funeral, each
returned home to California and Wisconsin, respec-
tively, and other than occasional Thanksgiving phone
chats and Christmas cards our families didn't indulge in
much contact after that. As it happened, my uncle never
spoke to me again after he heard about my arrest and
conviction as a forger. I never cared for the man, who
lived off the fat of his self-esteem but hadn't a tenth of
my father's drive, talent, instincts, or success. And as for
my aunt, I haven't heard from her in years and have no
idea whether or not she or any of her wearisome brood
are still denizens of the same planet as I.

For all his stiff-upper-lip demeanor, my father aged
pretty swiftly after Mom died. There weren't enough
trials to win or bibliographic rarities in the world to
buy that might fill the gaping void his beloved Nicole
left behind. Still, in the interim before I went off to
college—Yale, his alma mater—he did at times reach
out to me in the one way he best knew how, through

a shared world of books. While being a pathetic ruffian at school and obsessively focused on evolving my calligraphic skills at home, I read book after book. Novels, histories, poetry, drama, biographies. Every volume that wasn't deemed off limits in my father's library, as well as many that were, I devoured like some starveling who lived for his next meal. The last page and paragraph of one book led, often within the same several gestures and minutes, to the first paragraph and page of the next. Nor did I mix up any narrative with another. My memory was not eidetic, but it was as sticky as a fly trap. I went out of my way not to let others see this side of me, especially when I was young, as it is mysteriously clear to children that reading too much and remembering too well are often key to social disaster—especially if you prefer your mother's company. Not that I was by any means a social success. These skills did help me fly through college, though, and aided me in my earliest efforts as a legit book scout as well as inchoate forger.

When my father reached out, I reached back. He loved pulling down one of his treasured books and showing me precisely what distinguished it, what made it unique. His triple-decker set of Hardy's *Tess of the D'Urbervilles*, his *Emma* in original boards, his six-volume *Tom Jones* in contemporary speckled calf—each of these was in superb condition and, as he liked to say, "Fresh as the day they were born." Especially poignant to him was a book that looked just as it did on publication day decades or centuries before. Looked just as it did when the author held it in his or her hands for the first time. To possess a pristine copy was to share the author's experience, to virtually exist in another era as a time traveler might, and to join in communion with all those owners down the years who had protected it against time's depravities. That to him was the virtue of condition. Nor did his love of signed and inscribed copies have much to do with ordinary fetishism or pure market investment value, although he was both a good investor and surely a fetishist of sorts. Again, it had to do with proximity to the author. That the writer's flesh-and-blood hand had touched this title page or that piece of foolscap brought an immeasurable significance to the whole object. Made it distinctive and exceptional, yes, but, perhaps even more important, personal and even intimate. Authorial DNA, the scribed phrases and tender inscriptions, lifted even the commonest works into a higher category of value, not just monetary but, if you will, spiritual.

Some of our finest father-son moments had nothing to do with Little League baseball or going camping in the Adirondacks together, but rather took place whenever he got something special in the mail from London or Edinburgh or Paris. He would slowly unwrap the parcel with a look of both boyish excitement and mature satisfaction and then, after inspecting the rarity with ginger care, hand it to me. This was a little ceremony we both enjoyed, as well as an act of tremendous fatherly trust, I knew. I honored that trust by examining it with the deep shared interest of a newcomer learning from a master, before passing it back to its new owner.

"Book collecting," he memorably told me, though at the time I couldn't fully grasp his theory, "is an act of faith. It's all about the preservation of culture, custodianship, and that's why when I add a book to the collection I'm taking on the responsibility of keeping it safe. And then there's also the joy of the chase, of striving to find a copy of a book that helped make me who I am. But not just any copy—*the* copy, the most historically interesting and finest copy you can find. Most of all it's about something I've never quite been able to put into words. There's a line in T. S. Eliot's *The Waste Land*— have you read that poem yet?"

I shook my head, sorry I hadn't since I knew this was an important moment between us, one that I had better remember the rest of my life.

"Well, we'll read it together later. It's a line near the end that goes, 'These fragments I have shored against my ruins.' Books make us feel alive, and though we obviously won't live forever, they make us feel as if we might. These walls of books in this room? They stand between us and the unknown. And that's why I feel the safest and happiest and most alive right here. I suppose collecting anything is like that. Tin trucks, teddy bears, teapots. Things our ancestors made. We shore them against our ruins and they give us poor mortals comfort and joy just like religion does. Books are my religion, I guess you could say, Son. Not only the scripture but the religion itself."

I asked him, "What makes a book rare, Dad?"

"If I haven't seen it," he said, at first serious, then giving me one of his singular, warm smiles.

I was sixteen, my mother recently deceased, when he acquired what would prove to be a great triumph for him and a great temptation for me. Neither a book nor a manuscript but one of Conan Doyle's own pens that had come up at auction in London. Its provenance was indisputable; it was a thing of beauty. The pen, earlier than the Parker Duofolds Doyle famously used from the early twenties forward, instantly became one of my father's favorite items among the thousands in his collection. As he did with many of his acquisitions, he opened up the parcel in my presence and regaled me with details about what made it so special. But unlike so many other items that emerged from a carefully wrapped box, he didn't want me to handle this one.

"Look but don't touch." I remember his exact words and cautioning tone of voice.

I didn't understand, felt left out. It wasn't the most expensive piece he had ever bought, not by far. "Why? I thought you trusted me."

"I do. But we understand books, letters, manuscripts, and such. This is something different, like an excavated artifact from Mesopotamia, let's say, destined for a museum. We don't understand its fragilities and I don't want us taking any risks. Is that clear?"

"I won't touch it, promise," I lied, smiling up at him, studying the crow's-feet at the corners of his eyes as they flexed like courtesan's fans while he turned the lovely pen over and over in his large hands.

There are many moments, horrible ones and good as well, that I experienced with my father after we were left to our own devices, but this is one that I identify as a crossroads. I never liked lying to my mother because I loved her with such an open heart that deception, falsehood of any stripe, seemed not merely wrong but purposeless. My dad I venerated almost to the point of fear, on the other hand, at least throughout my early years and into my teens. So lying meant a promise of harsh consequences. Whenever I was suspended from school and I tried to blame the other guy for starting things, he would have none of it. To him, the inviolability of the truth, the authentic—both in his work and in his collecting—was paramount. In his practice, the man swam daily the polluted rivers of prevaricators, tricksters, perjurers, big fat liars.

"I don't want to come home to the same filth," he warned me.

It was a warning I mostly heeded—until the pen arrived from England. The idea of copying out or even composing a letter written by Arthur Conan Doyle using one of the author's own writing implements was too seductive, too provocative, and even lewd, if you will, for me to avoid. The indiscretion of the act only made it more desirable.

As if born to the task, I set about my innocent-enough betrayal with what in hindsight was something of a stroke of, well, genius might be too strong a word for it. Presumptuous ingenuity, let us say. Knowing my father's autograph archive backward and forward, I remembered there was an extra leaf at the end of a manuscript from the mid-1890s on which Conan Doyle had written only a number. He had, it seemed, finished the draft a page earlier than anticipated but left the final, mostly blank leaf where it was. This suited my purposes to a tee. Not only would I not be mutilating any of the author's original creation, but with the master's pen and a piece of paper he himself had touched, a vintage canvas, as it were, I could come as close to *being* Conan Doyle as anyone might.

Conveniently coming down with a cold on the same day that my father had to be in court, I found myself alone in the apartment for a goodly stretch of hours. I removed the spare leaf from the fancy leather portfolio that housed the manuscript—it was not attached with a pin or clip, fortunately—and set it before me on my mother's desk, where she and I had spent so many hours side by side in happier days. Painstakingly, I filled the master's pen with Waterman sepia and, on fresh bond, set about doing my practice doodles before signing "*A Conan Doyle*" a couple of dozen times. My hand was loose and confident. A kind of excitement the likes of which I'd never experienced rose in my chest, my pulse racing like a crazed metronome.

The next question was this. If I were to be Arthur Conan Doyle, it would never do to simply copy out something he himself had written. No, I needed rather to channel his voice, his ideation, his spirit. A sometime spiritualist himself, he would have admired this notion, so I told myself. I decided to write a brief letter on his behalf. It had to be simple, I knew, as I didn't have the necessary expertise to attempt a more complex text and have any chance at success. And what did I mean by success? I doubt I spelled it out to myself in as many words at the time, but the gist of the answer was plausibility. A plausibility of authenticity so strong that the document would convince even an expert as seasoned, hawk-eyed, and mistrustful as my hawk-nosed father.

After all of the possessions I divested myself of, I still own the fountain pen as well as this, my first forgery, and must confess I am as proud of it now as I was that snowy day years ago as a teenager in Manhattan. The letter was dated 1897, a year I chose after careful consideration. Written to the author's only brother, Innes, it begs off joining him for dinner—a banal background conceit that would ground my more intriguing addition, or enhancement, to the writer's life. The reason Doyle could not dine with Innes that evening was not because he had conflicting plans or had taken ill but rather because he had just met and fallen in love with a woman not his wife, and was in such a disquieted state that he felt it impossible to be seen in public. Her name was Jean Leckie, although in my letter Doyle guardedly gives his brother only a first name. She was beautiful beyond description. Young, vital, and of course altogether impossibly desirable. Although he desperately hated to say so, he confessed to Innes that should his wife, Louise, ever "slip the surly bonds of Earth"—my sole anachronism, and a fatal one had I ever tried to sell my forgery, as the line was written in 1941 by one John Gillespie Magee Jr., alas— he intended to ask Jean to marry him.

Our apartment library contained a number of biographies about Sherlock Holmes's inventor—indeed, we owned many books that weren't collectibles, dog-eared paperbacks and underlined reference books that were also well loved—and I was careful in my research to get my facts right such that the letter would not be encumbered by historical error. And but for that Achilles' heel of an exception, the inclusion of a flight of fancy phrase that would be a dead giveaway to any scholar who might study the letter for mistakes outside the realm of Conan Doyle's personal life, I succeeded. Writing out a draft on worthless modern paper, I then redrafted it twice more before setting nib—his once and now mine—to antique leaf, its wire-and-chain lines singing like lyre strings beneath the flowing words. After giving thought to how I might handle that page number, the one mark on the document that was in Conan Doyle's hand in fact, I decided simply to score the top half inch of paper with a razor blade, and then meticulously tear it away so the edge had a very slight fray. By rubbing the edge on the carpet of my father's study, I antiqued it with a hint of soil, aging the border just so. The small scrap with the number? I flushed it down the toilet along with my practice drafts, duly torn into postage-stamp-sized pieces. What else could I do with the incriminating thing?

Heart hammering, I looked at my little masterpiece in every different kind of light the apartment afforded—natural, fluorescent, filament bulb—and to my young eye it looked amazingly good. There, I thought. That wasn't so hard now, was it? I flushed and cleaned the pen before replacing it in the handsome leather box that housed it, a custom case lined with plush purple silk regal enough that it might have been suitable to the underdrawers of Queen Victoria, so luxurious and elegant was the fabric. Careful as could be, I returned it to the locked drawer where my father kept it and afterward replaced the skeleton key where he had hidden it—from others perhaps, but not from his watchful son.

I then needed a place to hide the forgery, for that's what it was, I proudly reminded myself. Hide it in plain sight, I thought, after looking around in my bedroom for a suitable spot and finding nowhere it might safely be stowed. Back in my father's library, I tucked it into the second folio volume of his set of Samuel Johnson's dictionary. No one, not even my father, would ever bother to look there. And, I figured, if someone did, well then, they would be delighted to discover a lost letter by Arthur Conan Doyle. Who knows but that it might even suggest that Doyle himself, or his doomed brother, Innes, once owned the book? It was, after all, perhaps the greatest dictionary ever written by a single individual, and in 1897 the committee-produced *Oxford English Dictionary* was not even halfway finished.

Outside, the snowfall diminished to a few confetti-like flakes floating down toward the street before finally stopping altogether. A brilliant winter sun that made the granite and bricks on the building across from our place sparkle broke through the clouds like some kind of celebratory celestial event. I am not making any of this up.

WHILE I NOW KNEW that my supposed Slader sighting was nothing more than a paranoid delusion, real enough to make me nervous and imaginary enough to make me unsettled, the fact that the police had brought him in for another round of interrogation truly angered me. My contentment and, much as I hated to admit it to myself, my safety were intertwined with his. Sure, I might once have been happy to see Henry Slader inconvenienced, messed with, disrupted in whatever possible way, but no longer. Leave the dog to his own devices and he would likely leave me to mine. So I found myself thinking, Why him? Why should Pollock bother with Slader, having to my knowledge not one substantial shard of evidence worthy of the word?

What had Slader been asked? What had he said? Had my name come up? If so, in what context? Above all, were they looking past Slader in my direction? I figured he must not have implicated me because, if he had, wouldn't the Montauk detective or some Irish proxy be at the cottage door to ask me a few questions as well? I had already been through a couple of long rounds of enquiry, very unpleasant to say the least. And though I wasn't a student of jurisprudence I had to think there was something akin to a statute of limitations when it came to questioning people, especially those who have rotated off the suspect list long ago, concerning whom no new incriminating evidence had surfaced. Not that any of these questions or self-assuring answers allowed me to sleep at night. Bottom line was, if Slader could be brought in again, so could I be.

Meghan noticed it before I did. "Your eyes," she said. "Have you looked in the mirror recently? They look awful."

"That's nice."

"No, don't get me wrong," she went on, her smile gentle. "I'm just worried that you seem so worried. You'll have plenty of time for bags under your eyes when there's a newborn in the house."

We were driving over to Kinsale for one of our foodie splurges, lunch at our favorite restaurant there, knowing that these forays of ours that dated back to the days when we were first together in New York, venturing on the subway to outer boroughs in search of the perfect hay-smoked duck wings or charred Korean octopus, were soon to become a pleasant memory. Infants neither like nor need hay-smoked duck wings.

"Worried, me? About what?" I never excelled at impromptu disingenuousness, but what had me in a twist was not even slightly within Meghan's purview and so she wasn't the wiser.

"About becoming a dad, of course," she said.

When Meghan said these words, our car flying along a narrow road overlooking the ocean a thousand feet below us, I caught my breath. Whether it was the concern in her voice or the bald simplicity of the statement itself, my future snapped into focus in a way it hadn't since arriving here. The granite-hard fact of fatherhood had never before registered at quite the depth I felt just then. Here I was in this old BMW we bought secondhand, driving on my new side of the road, the left rather than the right—I'm one who can find a metaphor in an empty teapot—which symbolized an entire new way of journeying forth through life. My wife sat next to me, a lovely, sensitive woman who had, for reasons that occasionally eluded all reason, fallen in love with and married me. I needed to let all the dead and living that I had gone out of my way to leave behind me remain behind. I took that wise thought and in my mind folded it into an invisible origami in the shape of a holy book, a book to live by.

The freedom I felt the rest of that day was revolutionary. Of course it would prove to be one of those fleeting life-is-but-a-dream moments. But it was as if a fever had broken. Sitting across from Meghan, indoors at the restaurant this time since the weather threatened rain and the purple and gray-green clouds raced each other across the sky, I felt I had never been more in love than that moment. Nor more at peace in years.

"My mother would have liked you so much," I said.

"So you've told me before," she replied. "I really wish I could have met her."

"When she died, I was too young to have had any kind of a mother-to-son talk about what kind of girl she hoped I would one day marry. But if I had to make that conversation up, I'd say you'd more than fulfill whatever hopes she might have had for me."

We drove back home in gusting rain, but if the sky had been a perfect cerulean blue, I wouldn't have thought it any more beautiful. I slept that night like the proverbial log. Life moved along with unwonted ease for a few weeks following my little epiphany. I would like to think that a kind of maturity settled over me, a maturity my mother had always worn with such grace, and as often as not, my father, too. And Meghan, who by this time had just begun to show a little, fairly glowed, looking for all the world like some Dante Gabriel Rossetti painting.

The certified letter that arrived just before Thanksgiving naturally made me jumpy. For obvious reasons, the mail and I would never be easy companions in the future, I who as a boy used to love it when the postman showed up, since as often as not he would be the bearer of rare books. I signed for it at the post office, although it was addressed to Meghan care of me. Studying the return address, I realized it wasn't from any of my demons but from my wife's old bookshop in the East Village. I hoped they hadn't gone bankrupt, since Meghan still owned nearly a third of the business. When she opened the envelope that evening before dinner, we discovered that quite the opposite had transpired.

"Looks like they're offering to buy me out," Meghan said, rereading the letter to make sure she correctly understood it.

I asked, "And how do you feel about that?" though I thought I knew the answer already.

"The timing is perfect, me being pregnant and all," she said, almost imperceptibly wistful. "Why hang on to it, since our life is here now, so long as we can keep our papers up to date. Right?"

She handed me the letter to read. Their offer was fair, as were the terms. Meghan, in any case, had remained part owner only in order to lighten the onus of their initial collective purchase. Bookshops were, are, and always shall be chancy, quixotic enterprises at best—easier to raise snow leopards in one's living room than keep an independent bookstore afloat—and that her erstwhile gang had made a sufficient go of it to come up with the cash to buy her out made her proud.

"I want to do this in person, sign the paperwork right there in old New York," she said, while we worked side by side at the kitchen counter, preparing a mishmash midweek dinner of leftovers. "While I can still fly and get around easily. Plus, let's have Thanksgiving there one last time, before the baby comes along."

Having made arrangements to be absent from our jobs and for the landlord to check on the cottage during our weeklong absence, we drove up to Shannon and caught a flight to JFK. Even though I had witnessed many a time the looming Manhattan skyline, that angular and pinnacled gray urban scape never resembled such an inert graveyard as it did to me during those minutes gazing out the taxi window as we neared the Midtown Tunnel. Meghan expressed great excitement to be back for a visit even though we had been away for only a little more than half a year. My excitement was counterfeit.

That same evening we had dinner at an Italian restaurant near Union Square with the bookstore staff, its soon-to-be-full owners, and as the wine flowed and plates of calamari and fried zucchini appetizers appeared, my spirits rose along with the rest. For a couple of fine hours I lost track of the infernal dread I experienced when we landed. I hadn't realized what a security blanket our secluded corner of County Kerry had become for me. Here, even surrounded by Meghan's delightful and adoring "kids," as she still fondly insisted on calling them even though a couple were her own age, I felt exposed, vulnerable, even naked. What made things worse was that I had—absolutely had—to hide any trepidations from my wife. If she asked, I would have no logical explanation for my foreboding.

Feeling flush, especially with the newfound money that would come from the sale of the balance of shares in the bookstore, we stayed at an unusually nice hotel overlooking my old neighborhood of Gramercy Park. The contract was to be signed and check cut on the Tuesday before Thanksgiving, executed at a lawyer's office down near Battery Park, and with no other business to tend to, Meghan and I visited her shop—"my old baby all grown up," she called it—one last time before shamelessly turning into holiday tourists. All those years we lived here, we had never visited the Statue of Liberty or the observation deck of the Empire State Building. We dined at La Grenouille and checked out the Central Park Zoo. Yes, I studied the faces in every crowd. Even aboard the old-timey Circle Line boat that circumnavigated Manhattan island down the Hudson, up the East and Harlem rivers, I found myself checking and rechecking my fellow passengers against the possibility that Slader or Pollock or anyone who struck me as suspiciously attentive might betray himself. But my Argus-eyed vigilance came to nothing, and Thanksgiving itself, which we spent in Providence at the invitation of Atticus and his family, promised the luxury of anonymity.

During Thanksgiving dinner, my longtime friend and colleague did give me a bit of a fright when he asked if he could have a private word with me while the supper table was cleared and coffee was being brewed to accompany pumpkin and mincemeat pies. I followed him to his study at the back of the rambling Victorian house on the hill adjacent to Brown University that he shared with his wife and two teenage girls, apprehensive as a buck in headlights that some forgeries from my collection had been returned to him, questions asked. Was it possible his hair had grayed a little more since the last time I saw him?

"I hate to put you to work on pilgrims' day," he said, pulling out a sheaf from the top drawer of an antique oak desk. "But I could use a pair of expert eyes, your expert eyes, on this thing I've been offered."

"No problem," I said, more relieved than he would ever know. "What is it?"

"I'm not sure whether you remember a Doyle story called 'The Cardboard Box.'"

Not only did I remember it but it happened to be one of my favorite of Conan Doyle's works because it was so unutterably dark, grimmer by far than most Holmes adventures. From the vantage of modern social mores, it wasn't such an unusual murder mystery. A spurned would-be lover, an adulterous wife, a violent alcoholic, a vengeful double homicide, physical mutilation, and Holmes in top form—what was there not to adore, was how I felt about it. The tale was published a little over a century ago, in 1893, on both sides of the ocean in the *Strand Magazine* and *Harper's Weekly*. Yet its author—so it was surmised—decided to forbid what I considered his most forward-looking, psychologically and physically violent, yes, but true-to-life story from inclusion in the London edition of his collection that came out later that same year, *The Memoirs of Sherlock Holmes*. He even went so far as to exclude any mention of the matter in his later volume *Memories and Adventures*.

"A draft passage," continued Atticus, "from Conan Doyle's autobiography, also suppressed or discarded it seems, has been discovered"—he held up the sheaf—"in which he reasons, point by point, why the story had to be omitted from *Memoirs*. And—get this—he adds some choice thoughts about his American publisher, Harper, who as you probably know didn't get the memo, if there ever was one, about the cut—which, it appears, pissed him off in the extreme. Doyle scholars out there have never been able to document definitively why he got cold feet about that story. Sure, people have had their theories going back for years. This," and now he extended the nondescript manila folder to me, "changes all that."

I did know the tale, both the fiction and nonfiction one, very well. It had interested my father, to be sure. If ever he had been offered what I thought Atticus Moore just handed me, I hadn't a doubt but that he would have bought it at all costs and considered the fallout later. The fallout being, of course, the strong possibility of sophisticated hijinks.

"I remember they had to withdraw the first American edition," I said, "and reissue it with just the eleven stories, with 'Cardboard Box' pulled out. My dad cherished his copy of the suppressed first."

"Damn rare book, no wonder he did. I have to confess it was one of the very first volumes that flew off
the shelf when I bought your father's collection. It's
safely tucked away in a special collections library now."
He saw the incipient look on my face and cautioned,
"Don't ask."

"Can I ask where you got this?"

Atticus laughed. "Still truffling for my sources, even
though you're out of the business?"

"Just curious is all."

"Well, you remember that scout named Henry
Slader? The one you asked me about a while back?"

"Sure," I said, noncommittal.

"I got this from a guy who, after working on him
for a while, coughed it up that he had bought it from
Slader."

My first thought was, as might be imagined, Slader
forged the pages that constituted a private record, re-
vealing at last Doyle's concerns about the story, its il-
licitness and strong insights into venal sin, immorality
in the first degree. But after I sat down at Atticus's desk,
asking "Do you mind?," and began studying Doyle's
words—he was frank in his assessment that the tale was
inappropriate for some readers, more sinister than the
Sherlockian brand readily permitted—I found myself
flummoxed, distressed even. Not so much because if
this were authentic it would constitute the holy grail for
any scholar interested in pinning down the author's ra-
tionale behind suppressing "The Cardboard Box" from
Memoirs of Sherlock Holmes, would provide convincing
written proof of what many critics over the years had
been forced to theorize, and that was the simple fact the
author got cold feet about the grisly tale of faithlessness

and murder he had set down on paper. No, what upset me was that Doyle's handwriting was perfect in every downstroke and pressure point, correct in every lift off of the nib and resetting on the paper. Above all, and far harder to fake, these sentences sounded like no one but the author himself.

"Well," Atticus asked, impatient. "Tell me. What do you think?"

"How much are they asking?"

He told me the number, in the thirty thousand range.

"Offer twenty and see what happens."

"But you still haven't told me what you think of the document itself. Is it real?"

"It's real enough. I'm holding it in my hands."

"Damn it, is it a forgery?"

For the first time ever—not the first time in a long time or the first time in a while—I hadn't a firm, objective answer to my friend's question. If Slader had crafted this, his skills as a forger were nearing mastery, or had fully arrived, I had to admit, and gone were the days of lesser works. If he hadn't, and this was truly an original, Atticus had himself a gold mine here. Either way, fake or not, I was deeply impressed. "If it is, it's the most perfect and interesting forgery I've ever seen. I'll tell you what's more. If I were still in the practice, I would be dying of jealousy over the quality of this work. It is pure as spring water."

Atticus was understandably frustrated by my assessment, I saw, and because we had been colleagues for so long and I had pulled the wool, in that unfortunate phrase, over his eyes on far more than one occasion, I settled on what to my mind was the truth of the matter. Or, truth enough.

"In my opinion, it's genuine," I said. "Congratulations, old pal. Looks like you have a lot to be thankful for this Thanksgiving."

He shook my hand, just a fraction of bemusement or concern or awe in his eye, I couldn't tell which, if any, and without having given it any forethought whatever, I asked, "You remember that remarkable cache of Doyle letters about *The Hound of the Baskervilles* you sold me a while back?"

"How could I forget? You got away with murder on that deal. One of the few things you hung on to when you moved over to Ireland."

"Well," I pressed ahead, "with the baby coming and seeing that you have this amazing find, maybe it's time I let it go. You want it back for the same I paid for it?"

I must admit that I myself was taken aback by the audacity of this impromptu idea. What was I thinking? Especially in light of the fact that two sets of these letters existed. But, I quickly reasoned, my set was more valid than Slader's because my forgery was superior. If Slader were ever to bring his on the market, it would be decried as a fake. A fake likely copied from my supposed original. The irony was exquisite.

"Are you sure?"

"I'm not a collector any more. What use is it to me to keep it? Let somebody else enjoy it."

"I can pay you a little more than you paid me, fair enough?"

"Nope. I'll take back exactly what I gave you and we can call it a day," I said. "I'll overnight it to you when we're back in Kenmare."

We shook hands on the deal and returned to the dining room, where our wives and his daughters—both of whom were champing at the bit to go to their respective boyfriends' family homes for dessert—awaited us.

"Big summit back there," said Meghan. "I hope nothing that will land either of you in trouble."

"Not him," Atticus said at the same time I said, "Not him."

"Well, that's a good start."

We sat down to our coffee and delicious homemade pies, along with some excellent cognac, before catching the late train back to New York.

Not surprisingly, on the ride down the darkened coast I obsessed over the documents I had seen in Atticus's study. Meghan nodded off, her head resting heavily against my shoulder, while I shut my eyes in order to visualize, with what memory was left to me in my middling years, Slader's—or, rather, Doyle's—diary. It was an exceptional find, if a find it was, and promised to fill in an intriguing lacuna in the Conan Doyle biography. I admired the thing, false or true, real or not.

Was it fair of me to think the document could be a forgery, albeit one of preeminent execution, solely because of its source? Probably so. Was it wrong of me to declare it the real article because it betrayed not a single flaw that I could see in the brief time I had to examine it, and thus provided me with nothing to point to as evidence of fakery? Probably not. This was a gnarly problem, one that left me perched on a very uncomfortable fence.

It takes a lot of truth to tell a lie. Truth must surround the pulsing heart of any lie for it to be convincing, believable. A pack of lies, like a house made from a pack of cards, will never remain standing. But a gracefully designed construction built on both visible and underlying truths had every chance of passing muster, of passing the test of time. As I used to do, Henry Slader might well be covering up his forgeries by handling legitimate works, first offering one and then the other to his clients, in a slow-motion sleight of hand. A wise way to proceed if less profitable. I realized I should have asked Atticus about provenance, just to see if he might not trip up and give me information I could use to cobble together the birthplace of this material. But, at the end of the day, I understood that provenance was every inch as moldable as the document itself. Give me a few hours and I will provide letters of authentication that might easily lift the questionable into the bright, hard light of sterling repute. History is subjective. History is alterable. History is, finally, little more than modeling clay in a very warm room.

One other matter perturbed me beyond my failure to be dead certain about my friend's documents. I had to admit to myself—since no one else would understand, with the possible preposterous exception of Slader—that I felt, how to put it, left out. Irrelevant. Here was my nemesis, actively engaged in a world with which I had always felt such an affinity, even in the darkest days when its populace temporarily exiled and loathed me. Now I was on the sidelines, a reluctant observer who was, as time passed, likely losing dexterity, muscle memory, and a thousand little refinements necessary to the art. Yes, I reminded myself, this was my choice. A good and sane choice at that. The magnificent woman asleep on my shoulder, in whose womb rested what society would view as my most meaningful creative accomplishment, was my guiding star. Any move other than to go with her to Kenmare would have been suicidal. And ridding myself of the Baskerville archive only underscored my determination to get out and stay out of the business, childish moments of feeling irrelevant aside. To continue to hang on to my last great forgery would have been like an alcoholic keeping a bottle of Dom Perignon in an otherwise empty wine cellar. What was more, I perversely liked the idea of sticking it to Slader, not that he would necessarily ever know. It was in many ways Slader's forgery, misattributed to Meghan's brother, that contributed to Adam Diehl's wrongful death. Best be rid of the hexed pages, especially in light of the fact that I knew Atticus would be safe selling them.

As the train pulled in to Penn Station, I gently woke up Meghan, feeling better, as if I had somehow dodged an existential bullet. I recalled the cautionary phrase popular in the world of recovering addicts—be careful of people, places, and things. Thanksgiving afternoon had confronted me with all three relapse triggers. I was grateful to push them aside.

Much as I wished otherwise, there was no avoiding a visit to Adam's grave. Feeling self-assured and as full of life as I'd ever seen her, Meghan proposed another field trip as well. "I can't believe in all these years I've never seen your parents' house in Irvington."

"It's been a long time since I've seen it myself. For all I know, it's gone through more than one set of owners and looks completely different from the days I lived there as a kid."

"One way to find out," she said. "Plus, aren't your parents buried near there? I think it would be lovely to go pay our respects before we head back overseas."

I have no idea why I hesitated. Her desire to visit my childhood upstate house and the cemetery that quartered my parents' remains was entirely thoughtful and typical of Meghan.

"If you prefer not, I'll totally understand—"

"No, no. It's very much the right thing to do."

"You're sure," she asked, which made me wonder what kind of look I had on my face.

"I'm all for it," I told her.

Montauk was first on the agenda. Meghan and I discussed whether or not it would be useful for us to try to meet with Detective Pollock.

"Makes sense," I said, having known for days this was inescapable.

"On the other hand, what could he tell us that we don't already know. Maybe we should make the visit just a family affair and not stir up bad memories."

"Myself, I wouldn't be sure what more to ask him, at this point," I offered.

"You're right," said Meghan, with conviction. "He knows where we are if he needs to reach us. Let's pay our respects to Adam, walk the beach a little, and get back to the city."

We rented a car for the weekend after Thanksgiving and drove out to Montauk after breakfast at the hotel. How to describe Adam's grave as having a "lived-in look" without sounding insensitive or glib? Obviously, these words never left my mouth, but unfortunately they were what came to mind as we approached the leaf-strewn, very slightly sunken plot. Someone had placed roses at the base of the headstone. They were very defunct now, and blossoms that appeared to have been pink once were now a brownish copper color. Meghan removed them and laid a dozen fresh white ones where they had been.

"I wonder who?" she whispered before starting tearlessly to weep.

"Could be anybody," I said softly, kneeling down next to her and placing my palm at the center of her softly heaving back. "Good Samaritan, I guess."

Together we hand-collected a couple of fistfuls of leaves strewn on the grass, stuffed them in the plastic bag we'd used to carry the fresh bouquet, and returned to the car. Meghan said that on Monday before we caught our flight back she wanted to call the cemetery folks and ask if Adam's grave could be regularly tended in our absence. "It should be better taken care of. I'll happily pay whatever fee they charge."

Seeing that her deep frustration over the openendedness of the murder investigation manifested itself in dissatisfaction with the cemetery management—in fact, the graveyard was, overall, handsome, tidy, and not at all disrespectful toward its necropolites—I kept quiet. Our walk on the beach was brisk and I could tell that Meghan's thoughts were every bit as stormy as the clouds that were piling up, nor'easter-like, along the purple horizon. It was rare that my wife ever stayed for long in a black mood. Whenever she was low, I had learned over the years, it was best to leave her to her own thoughts. She had ways of working through issues that I knew I would never comprehend, nor was it useful to try to push the wave faster toward shore. At lunch, while a light rain commenced, Meghan's usual demeanor returned. Over a couple of down-home lobster rolls, she did pose one disconcerting question, though.

"Who do you think that was back by the shore?"

"I have no idea what you're talking about," I said, setting down my roll on the paper plate.

"You didn't see him? Guy about your height, maybe a bit taller. Really short hair, pale, on the thin side?"

"What about him?"

"I'm surprised. You're usually the observant one," she said. "No, I'm just saying he seemed to be watching us, or you. I thought you might be friends."

I took a sip of water and glanced around the room to see if my friend had followed us here while he was at it. "Sorry, but I didn't notice him. I was more concerned about you, if you want to know the truth. Anyway, if he was a friend he'd have come over to say hello."

"Maybe he thought you were famous," she teased. "Lot of famous types out here on the East End, actors and financiers and the like."

"Famous is just about the last thing in this world I would want to be. Maybe you got all this wrong and he was staring at my beautiful wife. That's a far more likely scenario."

On the drive back in, I found myself wishing I had seen Slader, if Slader it was. My inclination would have been to toss caution to the wind, walk over to the man, and give him a piece of my mind. Fortunately, that opportunity didn't arise, as I could only believe that by provoking him I would bring further trouble upon myself. But how did he know we were here? Had Atticus inadvertently mentioned that I looked over his Conan Doyle materials at Thanksgiving and so tipped him off? It wouldn't have been a difficult stretch to guess that Meghan and I might visit Adam's grave, and with patience and nothing better to do I suppose he might have gotten some perverse pleasure in staking me out. To what end, I had no idea. More and more, the man seemed unhinged.

Our Sunday morning excursion up to Irvington— "headless horseman land," Meghan quipped—was less fraught, although we did have to drive past the exit that I once took on my first attempt to confront Slader in Dobbs Ferry. A nightmare I'd had right before waking up also hovered like a faint skein of mist around me. All that I remember of the dream were the words *Henry slayed her.* I dismissed the whole business, in part because if it had been Henry Slader on the Montauk beach the day before, I have little doubt he would have sidled up to us and said whatever he had in mind. He may have been unhinged but he was never shy about making demands. Anyway, the man owed me a thank-you letter if he had forged that brilliant "The Cardboard Box" material. Hadn't I proclaimed it to be authentic?

The old house looked surprisingly good. A classic brick Tudor whose upper story was fashioned of white stucco with traditional wooden crisscross decoration, the house had the same lead glass windows of my childhood, fronted by noble trees in orange, red, and gold autumn glory. Resembling a pen-and-ink drawing by the wonderful British illustrator Jessie M. King, it was grander than I remembered. Whoever owned it now had taken care of it admirably.

"Shall we knock on the door?" Meghan asked.

"No, that's okay."

"Come on, nobody would mind."

We did walk up the snaking path to the door and ring the bell, but no one was home.

"That's for the best," I told her, as we headed back to the car. "Too many ghosts better left alone."

"You don't believe in ghosts," she said, as we set off for the cemetery.

She wasn't necessarily right but I suddenly felt an urgency to get this visit over and done with. The family mausoleum housed my father's parents and other ancillary relatives I never met nor honestly much cared about. Interesting that I could write out from memory fairly detailed ancestral family trees for some of the authors whose letters I had forged most often but my own skeleton crew I barely bothered with. We didn't stay long, and as for the rest of our trip, it ended quietly with dinner for two in our hotel room.

The phrase *When you leave New York you ain't going anywhere* cycled around in my head during our flight back to Shannon. Whoever wrote that—I looked it up when we were back in Kenmare; Jimmy Breslin, a writer I had never read but recalled my father liked a lot—I appreciated the sardonic if heartfelt whimsy that informed it; the hometown narcissism that fed it; the Gotham greater-than-thou philosophy that underscored it. But for me, my embrace of the idea was of a different sort. I both wanted to leave New York and had no interest in going anywhere. Truth of it was, I had already been to more than enough *anywheres* for a lifetime. I was done with anywhere and longed to the core of my soul, assuming such a thing resided in me, for the great solace of a workable nowhere.

To be back in the cottage was to be back home. That was my first thought when I woke up, a little jet-lagged but eager to vault back into my life here, comfortably narrow as it was. Even the nostalgic sights of my upstate childhood house and the familiar streets of New York couldn't hold a candle to the quasi-tranquility I experienced in my adopted Kenmare, hand-grinding coffee in our quaint cottage kitchen, putting on my casual clothes to go back to work at the stationer's, consulting with Meghan where we should get together for lunch that day, should we order peat bricks, or rather turf, for the coming winter now that the November weather was turning nicely foul. Simple things like that.

Mr. Brion Eccles, owner of Eccles & Sons, Stationery and Print, knew of my proficiency with calligraphy even while he knew nothing of its dangerous incarnations in times past. No doubt it was one of the reasons he hired me, as early on in my tenure I was put to work executing handwritten wedding invites, baby shower announcements, citations, diplomas, whatever required a fancy script on some dull-as-dishwater document. I did these because I was asked to and because I think Meghan viewed the exercise as a positive use of my skill, if not a kind of rehabilitation. Although it was akin to asking a concert pianist to bang out "Chopsticks" on an untuned spinet, I diligently went about my business with nary a complaint. Having no nefarious scheme in mind, no thought of any future activity that might carry me back into my former hidden life, I did my best not to give in to schoolboy whimsy and scribe, say, a fiftieth wedding anniversary party invitation in King-Emperor Edward the Eighth's hand. I figured if Edward could abdicate his god-given calling for love, so could I.

It was, then, with restrained excitement on my part that Eccles pulled me off one of these somewhat galling calligraphy projects and asked if I could give it a try at working the Vandercook proof press he used for printing pamphlets, broadsides, and the like. He said his shoulder was aching, and because the press obliged the operator to crank the heavy roller holding the folio of paper across the type bed, back and forth, back and forth, he wasn't able to make a job deadline without help.

To say I took to it like a duck to water would be to employ a cliché—a lame duck of a cliché, at that— while understating an unimpeachable truth. I adored the smell of the viscous ink and tang of machine oil; adored the heft and smooth movement of the handle and roller; adored the repetitive sound of type lightly biting the skin of the paper. Above all, I adored seeing sheet after sheet of sharply printed leaves pile up. The textual contents of what I was printing became absolutely secondary to the act itself. I was reminded of my first writing lessons under my mother's tutelage, a watershed experience.

When Mr. Eccles thanked me for doing such a nice job, saying, "You're a quick study," I thanked him right back for the opportunity of running his press and offered to do it any time he needed me to in the future. "I may well take you up on that," he responded.

At home I announced, "I have news."

"Talk to me," Meghan said.

"Eccles had me run the Vandercook for the first time today."

Without a hint of sarcasm or irony, she marveled, "Apprentice no more. We have a Gutenberg in the family."

"Well, hang on. I doubt Gutenberg ever printed a four-up wedding invitation."

"'Four-up'? Listen to you, mister. You already sound like an old-salt pressman."

"He threatens to ask me to do more. Even said he'd be willing to teach me how to set and lock the type, clean up the press, from soup to nuts, if I was interested."

"Seems like you are."

"To be honest, I think it's a little bit of a childhood dream come true. As I'm afraid we both know all too well, the handwritten word's my first love—"

"Bad mistress more like."

I couldn't argue with that, so nodded before going on to say, "But typography and typefaces, my dad tried to teach me a little about them. He had sets of *Print*, a quarterly journal that was all about graphic arts and type, and another called *The Colophon*, from the thirties, just chockablock full of color illustrations, beautiful designs, and type treatments. Other kids had their picture books of Dr. Seuss and Babar and the rest. Me, I had something like four dozen hardcovers of *The Colophon*."

"Come on, you read *Cat in the Hat* and things like that."

"Only because of my mom. My father and I had loftier illustrated texts to concern ourselves with," I said, laughing along with Meghan. "Point is, I got to love those fonts. Bodoni, Caslon, Gill Sans. We even had a cat named Bembo. And old Eccles has trays and trays of this kind of type. I feel like a kid in a candy shop."

"You're a character. A true nerd."

"Nothing wrong with that, right?"

"I wouldn't love you so much if you weren't," she said, but then threw me off a little by adding, "Just don't go printing up any rare nineteenth-century poetry broadsides by Poe or Keats or something."

"Not funny," I shot back, with probably a far more snarling tone of voice than her comment had invited. What point would there be in lying to myself about the fact that this very idea had crossed my mind the first moment I set eyes on Eccles's proof press? Or, at bare minimum, printing up facsimile bookplates of collectible authors—an E. M. Forster or Edgar Rice Burroughs, say—to glue to the front pastedowns of others' books, thus making them into more valuable association copies given their estimable provenance. And yet just because I had expertise in one kind of forgery didn't mean I

could, let alone should, attempt to learn another. Great
painters don't necessarily make great sculptors, apples
are not oranges, and so forth. I struggled to soften my
tone. "Been there, done that. Or, I mean, been near
there, done something like that."

"Done and forever finished with that, too, right?"

"Meghan, drop it," I warned her, immediately ashamed
of myself for being so cross. I was defensive, of course,
and she was simply behaving like the protective, decent
wife she was, one whose concerns about her husband
were more than justified. Imagine what a dog's life
mine might have been without her. For her sake, for our
child's, I needed to stay on the path of probity as best
I could, needed to be not just a loving but a forthright,
honest man. So easy to say those words to myself and
at the same time so difficult, I knew, to live up to such
standards. I got up from where I was sitting, walked
over to her, and kissed her, saying in little more than a
whisper, "I'm sorry, Meg. I didn't mean to snap at you
like that. You don't deserve it, god knows."

The look in her richly blue eyes when she accepted
my apology—eyes the color of the earth's oceans as
seen from, say, the moon—made me all the more re-
gretful. I knew that I didn't deserve the love my wife
felt for me. But what was there to do about it now? My
sole course was to set any regrets aside, drown them in
the oceans of her eyes, and move forward.

Thanksgiving having come and gone, Meghan's
birthday was around the corner. I had kept up a tradition that started when I and, of course, Adam gave
her books by Yeats. Because I'd added a new volume
every birthday, she had a superb little collection of
half a dozen volumes. This year, for her first birthday

in Ireland as an adult, I needed something particularly special. Nor could it be a copy I jazzed up with some counterfeit inscription to Maud Gonne or Lady Gregory. Knowing it was impossible to buy one's way out of inextricable guilt, I still felt it couldn't hurt to make some gesture in that direction, and aware that Meghan's favorite Yeats poems were collected in his 1928 volume *The Tower*, I contacted Atticus and asked him to track down a first edition. It was not an inexpensive book, but I had plenty of credit with my friend and figured I wouldn't bother paying attention to the cost. True to his word, he located a beautiful copy in dust jacket and airmailed it to me the week before her birthday.

The stationer's shop wasn't far from the post office and, being excited about the book—Atticus told me the gorgeous T. Sturge Moore jacket was the sharpest he had ever seen—I dropped by every morning before work to see if it had arrived. Her birthday this year was on a Saturday and we planned, weather permitting, to drive to Kinsale to have a celebratory lunch at our usual place. Atticus's parcel arrived, along with another package for Meghan, on Thursday. Curiously, the second parcel had a shape and heft similar to the one containing my Yeats book. I took them both home that night and hid them from Meghan—not just mine, which I intended to keep secret anyway, but the other one as well. I knew it wasn't right to conceal mail addressed to someone else, be it spouse or stranger, but I needed time to think.

Something was wrong. No evidence one way or another, but I just sensed things were off. The label was typed, and not even on an electric typewriter but an old manual Royal or some other squat metal dinosaur

of its ilk. Who used manual typewriters anymore? Also,
the sender included Meghan's maiden name along with
her married surname, a ridiculously tiny detail that
nevertheless struck me as being amiss, or else taunting
somehow, reminding her that she was a Diehl still. To
what end, that? Above all, there was no return address
although the postmark was New York.

By the time Meghan got home, I had decided the package must be from the kids at her old bookshop. Only paranoia would suggest otherwise. But still I hadn't removed it
from its hiding place. Give it to her tomorrow, I thought.
No, better yet, give it to her on her birthday. I should have
been self-aware enough to recognize that I was postpon-
ing the possibility of trouble lurking inside the parcel.
During a sleepless hour or two that night, I even considered throwing it out. Who would be the wiser? When
the bookstore staff called to see if she liked her present, it
would become clear that it went astray in the mail. Sad,
but it happens more often than one likes to think. Was it
insured? Did they have the correct address? What was it?
Oh no, what a shame. Meghan, bless her, would undoubt-
edly say it was the thought that counts.

In the end, I neither destroyed nor looked inside my
brown-paper-and-string tormentor—yes, the package
was done up old-style. Instead, I wrapped *The Tower* in
beautiful pochoir gift paper that my boss had saved for
a special occasion, printed with hot air balloons and,
wonderfully if oddly, pachyderms in full regalia ridden
by pashas, also in full regalia. The book itself was a stun-
ner, a copy my father would have loved, and back in
the day I would have loved to improve it with at bare
minimum a signature. Aware I owed good Atticus more

than money for this, I brought my gift, along with the mystery package, to Kinsale.

We ordered quite a banquet. The weather held as we drove over, but then a rainstorm the likes of which we'd heard about in Ireland but not yet experienced set in on the coast. Drumming, thrashing water drenched everything outside.

"Look," I said. "We're dry and safe, not at sea. And plus it's your birthday. So I have something I hope you won't ever leave out in the rain."

Meghan was, how to put it, overwhelmed. Talk about a book nerd. Those earth-blue eyes of hers teared up.

"I love you," she said. "Thanks from the heart."

In retrospect, having just experienced what was as close to perfection in the generally flawed life we lead, or some of us lead, I should not have taken the chance. But I did.

"There's another present, or so I think, that came in from New York. From the kids."

She took the parcel, used a table knife to cut the string, and opened it.

"My god, this is wonderful," Meghan exclaimed.

It was a nice book for sure, a dust-jacketed first of Yeats's *The Winding Stair*.

"They pooled their shekels for that one," I said, relieved if at the same time surprised that they selected a volume whose design matched that of *The Tower*.

When she opened the book to the title page, everything good and hopeful went bad and sent Meghan into tears of a different kind. For myself, it sent me into a murderous rage, albeit behind as confused and concerned and benign an expression as I could manage.

The Winding Stair was inscribed in the poet's hand, the ink perfect, the placement on the page just exactly as Yeats would have done it, the lettering and signature impeccable, drop-dead impeccable, "To Meghan, on her birthday and in remembrance of things to come,

> *O body swayed to music, O brightening glance,*
> *How can we know the dancer from the dance?*

with all necessary affection, W. B. Yeats."

A SCRATCHING SOUND WOKE ME UP from my light sleep. Blurry after those several glasses of Irish whiskey I'd downed once Meghan and I arrived back home from Kinsale, I wondered if the stubborn sound, a rhythmic scrape-scrape-scrape, was real or else the after-echo of some bad dream, an already forgotten nightmare about digging a grave or clawing out from inside a coffin. Meghan was deep asleep—she was gifted that way, able to sleep no matter how upset she was when she laid her head on the pillow—her breath shallow and slow. The scratching seemed to come from out in the yard behind the house, insistent and though faint not in the least concealed. Whoever was there didn't care about being discovered. Brazen bastard, I thought, hearing also a light drizzle against the windowpane.

Weary, wary, and disgusted that what should have been such a beautiful day ended up with my wife furious and bewildered, and myself now convinced that Henry Slader was back, I slipped out of our warm bed, careful not to waken her. Listening as I went, I climbed down the stairs, which creaked and sighed with each footfall even though they were carpeted. I made my way by touch through the night-blackened rooms to the kitchen where, again as silent as I could manage to be without benefit of any lights that might warn him of my presence, I withdrew the meat cleaver from its slot along the side of the old butcher block next to the sink. Why, I thought, had I not bothered to keep a gun? Just as our landlord had offered to set me up with his grown son, who was a professional ghillie and hunting guide, so I could learn the basics of salmon fishing, he'd also suggested that I might like to try my hand at skeet shooting and even take one of his shotguns out after some waterfowl. I had nothing against fishing and hunting but just hadn't gotten around to taking him up on his kind offer. Standing there barefooted in the dark, holding a somewhat dull meat cleaver in my hand— something else I hadn't gotten around to doing was to sharpen it with the whetstone we had recently bought for the purpose—I felt like an impotent barbarian. Too, I noted my palms were damp with sweat even though the cottage was cool.

The scratching stopped for a time. Had the intruder heard movement inside the house and decided to skulk off, back into the anonymous night? How I hoped so. But then it started up again and so I blind-man-bluffed my way to the back door. Assuming that the sound was somehow coming from Slader himself—still in a

liminal state, I drifted ghostlike toward the switches for
the security lights and flipped them on, instantly flood-
ing the rear field with silver light—I was surprised to
see no forger, no human nemesis, nothing more than a
black-and-brown mongrel dog, hefty and mangy, vigor-
ously digging along the fresh-buried trench where the
electricians had laid their wires for the security system.
Furious, I stepped outside into the drizzle and shouted
at it, dropping the cleaver to clap my hands as I charged
the idiotic cur. He lifted his head and, seeing me coming straight at him, nonchalantly limped off into the
woods.

When I reached the spot where he had been digging, I could hear Meghan open a window upstairs in
the bedroom.

"What on earth's going on out there?" Her voice
combined alarm, irritation, concern, and, to be sure,
sleepiness. It must have been three in the morning, certainly the witching hour, and the wet grass was pain-
fully cold on my feet.

"There was a sound out here."

Even as I shouted those words back toward the
blinding lights of the house, unable to see Meghan in
the glare, I felt preposterous, like an insane person explaining why he insists on wearing a sideways Napoleon
hat and tucking his hand inside his ruffled blouse.

Meghan said something but I couldn't make out
what it was as I continued toward the trees where the
dog had been digging. With a flashlight I might have
been able to see what he had been trying to unearth,
but even with the security lights the hole was cast in
shadow, and I was disinclined to reach into it. Waste of
time, I thought. Can wait until morning. I headed back

toward the house realizing that I was soaked head to toe, my pajamas plastered to my body, my feet muddy. Probably looked like a bogman, or else some lousy mongrel myself.

Meghan was downstairs with a towel when I came through the back door.

"What was it? You must be freezing."

"You're going to laugh," I said, peeling off my soaked nightclothes and drying myself.

Meghan handed me my bathrobe and lit the burner under the kettle to make tea. "I doubt that. I'm not much in a laughing mood."

"Well, that's probably part of why I wound up outside. Whether or not you ever believe that I had absolutely nothing to do with that Yeats forgery, which, as I said over and over, was a cruel, thoughtless prank, I'm every bit as freaked out by it as you are. So when I woke up a little while ago because I heard a strange noise in the yard, my first thought was that whoever was behind that business might be back for more."

Meghan considered that while getting out chamomile tea and honey from the pantry. "Why didn't you wake me up?"

"You were so sound asleep, and after such a rough evening, I don't know. I can't say I was thinking clearly myself."

"So what was it? Really worth getting yourself soaked? Let's hope you don't get pneumonia."

"A stray dog digging away at something."

"Another hound of the Baskervilles?"

"Right," I smirked, and couldn't help but laugh at myself a little along with her. "Huge thing with monstrous red eyes burning like fire."

We had our tea and a rapprochement of sorts before
going back upstairs to bed. In the morning I called work
to ask if I could come in after lunch, as I was feeling a
little off.

"Late night," I explained, feeling guilty about making the request. After all, I myself had volunteered to
come in on a Sunday when the storefront was closed
so I could help do press work on the Vandercook, as
we were behind with printing orders. Being a good
Irishman, Eccles had no doubt forgiven an employee's
hangover more than once in times past. No hangover
or pneumonia either, my ailment, if such it could be
called, was a brute apprehension that Henry Slader had
managed to locate us and, riled by his newest interrogation regarding the Adam Diehl murder and my sale of
the Baskerville archive, had decided to exact reprisal.

But Eccles was talking. "How'd your wife like the
pochoir paper?"

"Loved it," I said. "She's saving it to reuse for the first
baby present."

"Good, good. Take the day, not to worry. Feel better."

While I dearly hated to miss a chance working the
press, I needed time to think about what to do. Besides,
I wanted to go out back and see what if anything that
dog was after, maybe look around the woods. Before
Meghan left to do some shopping, I couldn't help but
tell her, "Be careful, you hear?"

"What, you afraid a dog is going to bite me?" she
chided, reminding me, as if I needed reminding, that
my wife was nothing if not resilient. "Look," she went
on, "I'm really sorry that I went off on you like I did
last night. I was just shocked, is all, especially after your
beautiful present."

"Meg—" I interrupted, hoping we might avoid the dicey terrain of further discussion about the incident.

"No, listen. I should never have blamed you for that book. I know you had nothing directly to do with it—"

"Directly? Like I said over and over yesterday, I had nothing to do with it, period. Just because whoever did that knows a craft, call it, that I used to know, doesn't mean this rotten stunt has to do with me or my past. What I was trying to say last night, and probably didn't express myself that well because I was horrified by the inscription, too, is that there's every chance, and don't shoot the messenger, this has to do with Adam."

Meghan clasped her hands as if in prayer and brought them slowly and smoothly up under her chin. She was standing still as carved marble next to the front door, her heavy Aran sweater on, her string shopping bag hanging from her fingers like a forlorn miniature fishnet, ready to go to town. She started to cry again, quiet sobs. "It's just—how could anybody be so cruel?" she managed between breaths.

I was speechless, not because her question wasn't reasonable but because if I were given a millennium to sit in a whitewashed monk's cell and try to come up with an answer that was as reasonable as the question, I knew I couldn't do it. A cynical voice inside me said, Ask god, he's the one who started all this. Another said, Shut up.

The drear overnight clouds and drizzle had given way to tentative patches of blue sky, which in turn opened up as the morning sun burned bright. Outside, the grass was lightly blanketed in low-lying mist as rainwater in the drenched fields began to evaporate. A pair of magpies strutted across the misty lawn in the near distance and, farther off, a glossy chough performed impressive acrobatics in a yew tree. Finishing my cup of coffee, aware that I was putting off going outside to investigate, I finally pulled on my wellies and opened the back door. The air, its swirling little galaxies of fog having disappeared under the sun's strength, could not have been any purer than it was that morning. Disturbed by my presence, the two magpies protested with a noisy *chack-chack* as they lifted off and gracefully took wing over the wood's edge.

As I started across the lawn where not so many hours ago I had ventured forth like some fool in a bad horror movie, I thought of Slader, marveling at his intractable temper, his genuine madness. Yes, he would be upset if he found out about the Baskerville letters—and very likely he had, given Atticus's report of excitement in the scholarly world when they were sold to a library. If our roles were reversed, though, I'd like to think I would admire the pluck, not to mention the skill, it took to pull off such an antic. And yet he had gotten his pile of money, his pound of flesh. What further did he hope to extract from me?

Most concerning, the rest aside, was why do that to Meghan? Meghan who among all of us was the innocent. But then I remembered how much I had learned to dislike and eventually loathe Adam Diehl, to the point where I began to obsess about ridding myself of the man—forgers are superb obsessives, and because they disrespect the law, by definition they are dangerous obsessives—and with that, Slader came into better focus. A far superior forger than most, Slader was capable of deeper feelings of entitlement, the kind that made one feel very much at ease stepping into another's world and becoming, to the degree the act of counter-feiting allows such a metamorphosis, that person.

Listen to you, I thought, smirking as I walked. Phi-losopher of Kenmare pontificating to himself in his wellies. Still, for an enterprise that involves such a de-gree of education, sophistication, and civilized engage-ment, forgery does attract the uncouth brutish as well. Slader seemed to embody all those rudiments, and for that I had to grudgingly admire the man.

Even though the ground mist had largely burned off, I had to search around a bit for the hole the dog had dug. Just as well, in retrospect, because what I found moments later would mark another turning point in my life, an abrupt precipice I might sooner have wished to avoid.

The hole was not that deep, just half a foot, if that. It wasn't deep because it wasn't intended to be deep enough to thwart the dog, not just the dog I witnessed but any dog, from digging up the bloody gloves that were deposited there. I gasped, or think I must have, and before examining them closer peered around me, squinting, to see if anyone out in the woods or back at the house was watching. Seeing no one, I knelt down. Made of natural calfskin and drenched in blood that was only partly dried, the gloves resembled a pair of dis-membered hands. Human blood? No, this is a country where people eat blood pudding and the like; butcher shop blood is come by easily enough. Repulsive none-theless, and whoever set the gloves here had even gone to the trouble of stuffing their fingers and wrist with mud and shanks of grass, for verisimilitude. The dog had managed to chew off one of the thumbs before I'd come outside and scared it off. Most disturbing of all, at least at the time, before I had a chance to absorb what was going on here, was that a round-headed spike had been driven into the gloves at the wrists presumably to hold the thing in place. In other words, I was meant to discover this travesty. Had Slader—for it had to be Henry Slader—even brought the mongrel along in order to set the discovery in motion? Looking around again, I noticed a large bone lying in the grass at the wood's edge, most of its meat gnawed off. Was it placed with the bloodied gloves as bait and dropped when the dog bolted?

Leaving the gloves where they were, I traipsed out into the thicket, which remained quite wet, shaded as it was from the sun. I hadn't much hope of finding anything further—indeed, didn't want to find anything, given how unsettling was the discovery I had already made—and didn't. Any footprints, human or canine, were erased by rain. Nor did I possess the kind of deductive intuition that a Sherlock Holmes would have exploited to interpret this broken branch or that scrunched leaf. Phrenology of rustic woodlands, so to say, was never my strong suit and, as such, I gave up my dismal, halfhearted search and reluctantly returned to the gloves.

A more damning, insolent, yet insanely eloquent accusation couldn't have been made, even if it had been written in large condemnatory block letters. You murdered Adam Diehl. You dismembered him and left him for dead. Now you're content to let me take the fall?

How I wished I could speak with Henry Slader for a calm minute or two. Let him know he had things added up wrong. Sure, I bested his Baskerville forgery, big deal, but I had nothing whatever to do with the

Montauk police's interest in him. It was his own dealings with Diehl that persuaded them to seek him out.
But of course the time for such a platonic dialogue, two
respectful souls conferring, not only was long since past
but was never, ever fated to be. There was nothing to be
done about it. Nothing I could think of that morning.

I had no choice, meantime, but to hide the mess before Meghan got home. Fetching out a few plastic bags
from the mudroom of the cottage and putting on a pair
of my own gloves so I wasn't forced to touch anything,
I returned to the hole and withdrew the long nail. The
calfskin gloves I pulled free of the stake, dropped them
into one bag, and tightly cinched it up. Then I double
and tripled bagged it. Carefully, I kicked the loose
caked dirt over the shallow cavity and tamped it down
with my boot. On Meghan's return, I would simply tell
her that I wandered out to have a look-see and found a
partially chewed bone that must have been the object
of the hound's persistent interest. The plastic bag I hid
beneath some mildewy burlap bags in the cellar, and as
for the long nail I washed it clean of dirt and blood in
the slop sink downstairs. Seeing that it looked like new,
the most innocent stake ever to wink under the light of
a bare bulb in a County Kerry cellar, I dried it off and
burrowed it under a whole array of nails in a box on a
workbench shelf.

Having showered and seeing that Meghan hadn't yet
returned, I decided to make us lunch, maybe recapture
some remnant of the joyful married camaraderie we'd
shared in Kinsale before the imposter Yeats—now ban-
ished to an unused cabinet drawer in an equally unused
room—reared its ugly head. I set the table with our
fanciest plates and silverware, got some soup going on

the stove. Opening a tin of smoked kippers and toasting some thin-sliced bread, I boiled a few eggs and made up a quick cucumber salad. Self-consciously and perhaps unnecessarily, I placed Meghan's copy of *The Tower* on her plate, a reminder that one of her presents was real, was given with affection. I planned on confessing to her that the reason I had Atticus locate a copy without a signature or any inscription was precisely because I wanted her to know it was unadulterated, unquestionable.

When she did arrive home, I helped her bring in the groceries and other sundries. She was delighted by my modest surprise lunch, although I could swear I detected the slightest distance in her demeanor and language. A distance so slender it wouldn't have been noticed by anyone other than me. I assured myself she was still upset. And why shouldn't she be?

"You figure out what your Baskerville hound was after last night?" she asked, setting her book on the sideboard and sitting down to eat.

"I did."

"And, Sherlock?"

"Doggy wanted a bone, it seems," and told her what I had found, the part that she needed to know, that is. "I left it where it was."

"No, don't do that. We'll be up in the middle of the night again when it comes back looking for the thing."

I agreed, knowing the sole reason I'd left it where I found it was in case Meghan had any desire to see for herself that the mystery was solved. After lunch, I went back outside by myself carrying yet another plastic bag and collected the calf femur, as I imagined it was, to bring back inside and toss in the trash. Purplish clouds were collecting over toward the west, promising another night of rain typical for the season. Walking back, I saw Meghan in the upstairs window, watching me I couldn't see the look on her face but when she waved to me I could swear there was a mechanical stiffness to it, an obligatory gesture that wasn't informed by the confidence and love I had grown so accustomed to seeing in my wife's everyday moments. I waved back, rather too heartily I suppose. Likely trying to make up at my end the passion I found missing at hers.

This was going to be temporary, I knew. Still I couldn't help but feel downcast. And now walking somewhat more tardily toward the cottage, my eyes lowered, I realized that the cleaver I had dropped on the grass when I chased after the dog last night was gone. I glanced back up at the bedroom window and, noticing that Meghan had withdrawn into the cottage, searched everywhere for the cleaver, to no avail. Not wanting to be asked what I was looking for, I gave up and went inside. I dropped the bone into the garbage bin and quietly, quickly looked all around the kitchen on the off chance Meghan had brought it in. But no. The cleaver was gone. Never, I hoped, to return.

MEGHAN THOUGHT WE SHOULD take the book to the police, which was, naturally, the last place I wanted to go.

"What would the complaint be?" I asked. "I'm not even sure that whoever did this committed a crime beyond ruining your birthday and what used to be a damned nice Yeats book."

"The inscription's a forgery," she argued. "If anyone ought to know that's against the law it's you."

Ignoring her barb, I said, "That's true, but in this case the forger didn't try to sell you the book. He gave it to you, and there's nothing illegal about that, I'm afraid."

"Don't you think it's kind of threatening, the inscription?" she persisted, probably knowing as well as I did that there was no concrete reason for us to bother the Kenmare sergeant with what surely was a private matter.

"Please don't get mad at me if I tell you that while, sure, you and I don't like the tone of it and feel there's something wrong, an objective interpretation could just as easily suggest it's perfectly friendly. 'With all necessary affection'? 'Remembrance of things to come'? A famous couplet from one of Yeats's most famous poems? I can hear them asking us, Where's the threat? We're just settling in here, and I for one don't think we ought to bring attention of this kind on ourselves."

Meghan frowned, but it was a gently discouraged frown that made it clear she found herself agreeing with my points. After a moment, though, she did say something I had not thought of. "By the way, did you happen to notice that the poem he's quoting is not from *The Winding Stair* but *The Tower*? What are the chances of that?"

She was right. A fine prickle of electricity bolted its way down my spine. I needed to make a couple of phone calls. First, I had to ask Atticus whether he had mentioned anything about my purchase of *The Tower* to Henry Slader, and if so—or, for that matter, if not— for godsakes never to mention any of my doings to the man in the future. Consider him my enemy, I planned on informing my Providence friend, though not in so many words. Second, I wanted to speak with a bookseller acquaintance up in Dublin who specialized in works by Irish writers, Yeats chief among them, see if he or any other dealers happened to have sold a copy of *The Winding Stair* recently. I didn't want to call Atticus in front of Meghan because I didn't want to further alarm her and, more to the point, needed to stave off

letting her in on Henry Slader's confounding relationship with me for as long as possible, hopefully forever.
Slader could rip open my fragile world if and when it
pleased him, it was becoming all too apparent. I needed
time to figure out how to preclude that from happening, and scolded myself for having had the hubris to
sell my Baskerville archive at Thanksgiving. That was a
dangerous bit of immature roulette I might have spared
both Slader and myself.

"I don't know the answer to that," I said. "But I agree
it's weird. Look, I can tell you where I bought your
present if you want. You'll see he's a friend and that
there's no way he was in cahoots with whoever sent
The Winding Stair. Either way, I don't think it's going to
answer your question, any of these questions."

Meghan, as if realizing suddenly that I hadn't
wronged her, that I had given her a beautiful book spe-
cifically without suspect handwriting in it—didn't even
pencil in a happy birthday wish on the front flyleaf—
found her smile again, the smile I loved so much, and
said, "I'm sorry, I think I've been taking some of my
upset about this business out on you." She walked
over and wrapped her arms around me. "I don't need
to know where you got my lovely *Tower* and we don't
have to do anything about that other one. Who knows,
maybe the kids at the shop are behind it and the whole
thing is innocent as angel food cake. They could have
hired somebody to make a decent facsimile of Yeats's
script and they worded it a little clumsily and meant no
harm whatsoever."

Drawing her closer, I could feel the slight bulge of
her belly. I proposed in a voice as comforting as I could
summon, "That's how we'll look at it unless we find

out otherwise," knowing even as I spoke that her con-
jecture might have had the weight of possibility, even
probability, on its side but for the fact that *The Winding
Stair* was a volume worth a couple thousand dollars at
least. Or it was before the spurious inscription ruined
it, turned it into a sickening curiosity. It was surely beyond the means of Meghan's former staff who, at any
rate, needed all their pennies to keep the shop afloat.
No, who sent it meant to make a very clear, very serious
statement—and, I knew, it was a statement intended
for me more than my guiltless wife. I further knew, but
no way was I going to tell her, that only an artisan of
the highest order could have produced that inscription.
One doesn't just hire some everyday calligrapher off
the street and hope for such perfection. Grudgingly, I
had grown to admire Slader as much as I hated him.

My chance to call Providence came the next day
while Meghan was at work. Taking my lunch break half
an hour early with the excuse I had left my wallet at
home, I drove back to the house and telephoned Atticus. Sure, if Meghan wanted to check she would be able
to see it on the phone bill, but my need for privacy was
less because I called my friend than that I didn't want
her to hear what I needed to ask him. Fate was on my
side, as he picked up after a few short rings.

"So how did *The Tower* go over?" he asked, immediately. For a bookman as obsessed as Atticus, books
always came first, the social niceties of enquiring how
things were, how's your health, all that congenial riga-
marole, invariably taking a back seat.

"She loved it. I love it, too. Best copy I've ever seen."

"Not a hint of the usual fading on that dust jacket,
right?"

"Plus, the gold stamping on that binding underneath is bright as can be, blindingly so."

"I told you it was a honey of a copy."

"Well, I always said you're a wizard. Thanks for finding it, Atticus, and like I said, just take whatever I owe you off what you owe me."

"Already done."

"Good, good." Knowing my time was tight, I pushed forward, saying, "I have a kind of delicate question I need to ask you and hope you don't mind keeping it to yourself. And don't worry—" I anticipated him, "it's not about forgery or anything of the kind."

"Go on," he said, with crisp Yankee brusqueness.

"We've talked about Henry Slader on occasion, and you were saying at Thanksgiving you've done some business with him."

"Right."

"I was just wondering if by any chance he happened to ask about me?"

Atticus Moore was a longtime friend, and I could always tell, even at a distance of several thousand miles, when he was disinclined to discuss something. A pause that went a beat too long, a modified tone in his voice. "Why do you ask?"

"Well, to be honest," I said, quickly inventing a half-truth, "Henry and I had some dealings in years past that went south. Somebody I was talking to mentioned that he was still bad-mouthing me about it, and I wondered if he said anything to you."

"Oh," Atticus said, audibly relieved. "Nothing of the kind. He heard about my reacquisition of those Baskerville letters and made the journey to Mecca to see them for himself. I told him I planned on trying to sell them in tandem with the materials that came from him through another source. He was nothing but laudatory about both the archive and you. No bad-mouthing in the least."

"I guess you must have told Henry you bought the Baskerville from me?"

"No need. He already seemed to know. I assumed you told him since he spoke so warmly about you. Asked how you were and about Meghan. Guess he knew her brother Adam quite well, he was saying. I think they were close."

Tucking that odd last revelatory bit away to ponder or not some other time, I pressed on. "Did he ask where we're living?"

"Oh, I hope I didn't speak out of place. But yeah, I told him you were loving Ireland and had found a great place to live off the beaten track. It really all couldn't have been more friendly and innocent."

"No, I'm sure it was. That comes as a relief, then, that the rumor I heard was false."

How dearly I wanted to ask Atticus if Slader knew I had purchased *The Tower* from him but I assumed he did, given the charming-like-a-fox geniality Slader had mimicked in order to get information he needed about me, my wife, our whereabouts. I wouldn't have put it past the tawdry bastard if he even bought that doomed *The Winding Stair* from Atticus. Fell into the did-not-need-to-know category.

"One last thing, though, Atticus."

"Talk to me."

"If Henry or for that matter anybody else comes around enquiring after me and Meg, I would like to request you just play ignorant. We're trying to start a brand-new life here after all the heartache we've both experienced and you're one of the only people we want to be in touch with. You and the kids at the bookshop in New York. Hope you understand."

"I respect that," he said. "Sorry if I was a little loose-lipped with Slader. Didn't seem at the time there was any ill will, quite the opposite. But we're good. How're Meghan and the little one on the way doing?"

"Fine, wonderfully," I said and we finished the conversation on a very cordial note, although the minute I set the phone down, I bellowed at the top of my lungs a string of angry obscenities, directed at everybody, at nobody, mostly at myself. Slader knew everything. And Slader was here. That second call to Dublin I didn't bother with. Whether *The Winding Stair*, a stair down which I wished I could shove Henry Slader, came from Providence or Dublin or Timbuktu didn't matter any more. I had serious trouble on my hands and no good move to make.

Back in the stationer's, I did my best but failed to keep my mind from wandering away from my work. Meghan had stopped by during her lunch to find me gone, and was told I'd gone home and why, so went about her business with the tacit understanding I would drop by at the end of my workday as usual. Eccles had me running the press, which was for the best given that it kept me in the back room, away from our customers. I couldn't be sure I would be able to disguise my dismay about what I saw as an inevitable confrontation, and, besides, the repetitive labor involved with working the Vandercook had a meditative effect, cleared the mind at least temporarily. As a result, the afternoon hours quickly melted away, and sooner than expected my boss told me it was closing time. I cleaned the press, stacked the finished sheets neatly on the worktable, made sure the tins of ink and solvent were closed, and went to the bathroom to wash up.

Walking past the small industrial guillotine we used to trim business cards, menus, invitations, and all of our other print jobs, I thought of Adam's missing hands and the accusatory bloody gloves recently planted in our yard. What I felt was not fear or shame or inspiration or anything as emotional as all that. Numbness might best describe my feelings at seeing the sharp blade that we used almost daily and which, for whatever reason, I hadn't much thought about before. In the bathroom I shook my head while soaping my own hands and rinsing them under a stream of very hot water. Fortunately, there was no mirror in the employee restroom. I wouldn't have liked to see the look on my face just then. Not that I know what my demeanor might have been. Whether a scowl or smile, I didn't need to witness it.

I dried my fingers, knuckles, palms, wrists, and held them before me. Mad as it may sound, I considered them, fronts and backs, for all the refined work they had accomplished over the years. All of us, I realized, had done very bad things with our hands, even those whose lifetimes were largely spent laboring in the sunnier fields of ethical goodness. Mine were just another such pair, with acts virtuous and sinful in their past. What they might do in the future I couldn't know, although I swore that because of my wife and our coming baby I would do everything in my power to restrain them from erring in some destructive direction.

Outside, a south wind freshened the already nippy air. It tasted a touch of tidal brine as it often did, I had

noticed, before rainstorms came in off the Kenmare
River, a bay estuary where the freshwater Roughty
meets the salty Atlantic beyond. I shoved those hands
of mine, still warm from the faucet water, deep in my
jacket pockets and strode down to the post office—no
letters, thankfully—then up toward the bookshop. Unlike days past, I didn't bother to look over my shoulder
or search the pedestrians ahead for a face that should
not have been as familiar as it was, given how few times
I had actually met Slader. He would present himself
when he felt it was opportune to do so, and since there
was nothing I could logically do about it, I thought it
best to conserve my strength by not devoting further
energy to the matter.

Instead, I dropped into a charming little boutique
of handmade women's clothing where Meghan often
stopped us to window shop whenever we happened by,
and bought her two beautiful scarves—wool for winter
soon upon us, silk for spring to come—intending to give
them to her for Christmas. As the shop girl began to
wrap them, though, I changed my mind and asked her
not to use the holiday gift paper but just some plain
silver foil they had.

"It's for a birthday, not Christmas," I needlessly
added.

Walking more briskly now, because I was running
late and also the wind had picked up, I decided that
tonight would be a surprise second birthday party, one
that would make up for Saturday's debacle and the
crazy-making nocturnal disturbances that followed. So
much of what stability and happiness I possessed came
directly from my devotion to Meghan, and hers to me.
Hairline cracks in the usual fortress-strong wall of her

affections for me seemed to have widened a little recently, or so I had perceived them. To say the least, this
worried me. No, I needed to admit it terrified me. Without her I would be lost, bereft, and I knew it. Not that
I could bandage those ostensible cracks with a couple
of scarves no matter how pretty they were. Still, I felt I
had to do something to smooth things over.

She was standing, arms crossed, on the front porch
of the bookshop, which was in a house set back from
one of the main roads in town.

"You have a girlfriend or something, mister?" she
asked, not entirely joking.

"What?" was all I could manage.

"Well, you weren't at work during lunch break when
I came by. They said you had to go home to fetch your
wallet, which I know you had on you this morning be-
cause you gave me money when we got to the village.
Now you're late to pick me up and you're never late.
Seems like you have some explaining to do."

Relieved, I laughed, handing her the shopping bag
from the boutique. "I'm late because I made a quick
stop at Eileen's to get you another birthday present,
which, if you'll allow me, I'd love for you to open at the
restaurant of your choice tonight. And it's true, I lied to
Eccles about my wallet because I wanted to go home
and phone Atticus about that *Winding Stair.* As for a
girlfriend, I already have one and that would be you.
Do I hear an apology?"

Meghan's face changed, its hard edges softened, the
tightness around her lips relaxed. It was as if subtle light,
like that of a waxing moon, suddenly illuminated her
from within. She thanked me for the present, assured

me it was entirely unnecessary, and apologized more earnestly than her harmless accusation warranted.

We were fortunate to get a table near the open fire in our favorite pub—well, we had several by this time— the rain having started coming down in steady gusts before we arrived. Nothing fancy like Kinsale, here we dined happily on clam chowder and fish pies. Meghan's mood had, it seemed, returned to normal, and when she asked me what Atticus had said about the Yeats book, I truthfully told her he knew nothing about it—knew nothing because I hadn't mentioned it, yes, but my answer was honest enough. After a second pint, I entered a pocket of time in which life seemed good, secure, not threatened by the past or "things to come." I knew I had been living on a kind of sine curve, a rolling wave of ups and downs, now hopeful now doomed, now asleep now insomniac, now cocksure now deeply uncertain. If such a roller coaster of moods and dispositions had taken its toll on me, I thought, imagine what it must have been like for Meghan in recent months.

When my wife excused herself to go to the ladies room, I found myself staring at the prancing citron and orange flames in the fireplace and made a decision I truly aspired to hold myself to fulfilling. If—when— Slader approached me for another round of hush money, other than kill him, which I had no intention of doing, what could I do but somehow pay it without complaint and expeditiously as possible? It occurred to me that I could transfer all further income from Atticus Moore's sales of my father's books—only about half of which had sold, and many of those purchased on time payments stretching out for as many as a few years—to an account I could open without Meghan's knowledge, one from which I could in turn pay Slader. That would be a goodly sum, enough for him to buy himself other obsessions besides me. I could also promise Slader I would never cross him again, although I doubted my word would carry weight. Twice burned and all.

Mesmerizing as the lively fire was and calming as was the stout, I understood this might not be sufficient to rid myself of the man. But at least, I thought as Meghan returned and took her seat, I had my response in place when he came calling. Over coffee, Meg finally opened her presents, which she loved so much she wore them both home that night wrapped around her graceful shoulders and neck.

His letter arrived at the post office the next day, as punctual as if it were scheduled on some malign calendar. Oblivious to the cheerless damp morning weather, to the leaden sky stretched low and claustrophobic overhead, I sat down on a public bench in the village square and read it on the spot. Its lack of greeting or signature at the end were all too familiar to me by now, and that it was scribed in W. B. Yeats's hand rather than that of Henry James or Arthur Conan Doyle was equally routine. None of it nearly as disquieting as Slader's earlier letters had been back in the day when I had no idea who I was dealing with. These expected details aside, the letter offered nothing by way of comfort, nor was it so intended.

What is a dead poet to do with you? You have created with your greed and craziness a problem that requires

*resolution. This is your own doing. You had your chance
to leave us squared away. But you do not seem to appreciate the honor of surrendered defeat. In my kindness,
I can try to spare you and your family one last time. My
instructions will arrive soon. Follow them to the letter unless you want your baby to be raised in an asylum for
foundlings.*

No Yeats, but the man did have his way with words—
although, rather than wince at that final antiquated
image, I sneered at its self-importance. Most aggravat-
ing was that his instructions would "arrive soon." Why
not now, why dally? Was Slader merely a sadist or had
he not yet figured out what he wanted from me? These
questions were as baffling as they were frustrating, yet I
clung to my earlier pact with myself to remain as calm
as I could under the circumstances and react only when
the situation presented itself.

That afternoon when the stationer's closed, I went
home rather than wait the hour or so for the bookshop
to close. Meghan told me she wanted to walk, get some
exercise for herself and the unborn. "Too much yummy
fattening pub food," she joked that morning at the
breakfast table. I told her I would see her at home, that
I had some straightening around the cottage I wanted
to do, maybe read a bit.

As I pulled into the drive, I thought I saw that black-
and-brown mongrel out at the edge of the field, a yard
or two in from the tree line. Son of a bitch, I thought,
and considered grabbing a rock, nonchalantly strolling out there, and, when I was close enough, hurling it
right at his insouciant head. Put him out of his misery
and mine, too. But I thought the better of it, turned

the engine off, and withdrew inside, carrying a paper
bag with the can of solvent I had borrowed from work,
locking the front door behind me. I shuffled out of my
trench coat, knocked off my muddy shoes in the foyer,
and went straight downstairs to rummage out those
gloves. After carefully pulling away the burlap that
concealed the plastic bags in which I'd hidden them,
I was dismayed to find that the bittersweet, acrid odor
of death, however faint, lay in the still mildewed air.
Taking the bags over to the slop sink, I set to scrubbing
out the caked red-brown blood staining the calfskin.
I never intended to use them, of course, but when I
threw them away in a public receptacle, as I planned
to, I wanted them to be as cleansed of telltale blood as
possible. Not, of course, that this particular blood had a
tale to tell that anybody besides Slader and I, unwilling
and loath conspirators, might ever decipher.

They cleaned up better than I'd anticipated, and
more quickly, as did the plastic bags, although they now
smelled of solvent, which, after running them under a
stream of alternating cold and hot water, also dissipated.
I dried off my hands after wiping down the metal sink
and headed back upstairs. Another plastic bag from the
kitchen, a furtive scan out the back window to see if
that mangy mutt still skulked around—seemed to have
disappeared, good—and soon enough I was back in the
car, this time driving across Cromwell's Bridge away
from town, to a small marina on a fjord-like lake whose
water glistened like India ink. Meg and I had come here
once on a ravishing midsummer day to watch the wind-
surfers in their gaudy-bright wetsuits tacking surreally
back and forth. That day the dock was crowded, the
parking lot by the shoreline full. This evening, no one

was about and I made my rather innocent deposit in the nearest covered trash bin. Before driving back to the cottage, even though time was tight and Meghan would be home soon, I took a moment to breathe the sweet, mist-rinsed County Kerry air deep into my lungs, inhaling with the lusty urgency of a terminally ill patient. I breathed in and out, assuring myself as I did that things would work out, life would settle into a routine of domesticity and parenthood and calm. Then, a bit lightheaded but sharp enough to drive, I made my way along the winding, tree-canopied road back home.

Like some family pet, the mongrel was sitting on the top step of the front porch when I swung back into the drive. My headlights caught his eyes which, startlingly, shone silvery white, or like mercury, eyes that were empty holes. More defiant than fearful—he had never come after me, only shuffled away when I'd shouted—I got out and slammed the car door shut, assuming that would frighten him off. Oddly, it didn't. As I walked toward the porch, I realized that any ire I felt toward this dog was misplaced. He held his ground until I was close enough to either pet or else kick him, and finally snarled at me, warning that I do neither. When I saw he was lording over a slab of fresh meat that was set before him, circumstances became clearer. Dumb pawn, I thought, and looked behind me, scanning the gloaming fields and back up the driveway.

A figure was walking my way, I saw, a hundred yards off on the dirt road that led to the drive.

"Meghan?" I shouted, hopefully. Seeing that she seemed not to have heard, I turned back to the dog and said, quietly, "What can I do for you?"

Almost as if he understood or made his move on cue, the beast snatched up his hunk of beef or lamb or whatever it was and walked, then loped, then sprinted silently across the lawn, disappearing into the forest.

I turned once more to glance down toward the still indistinct figure coming closer, and called out again, "Meghan?"

"Hey," she cried back, her voice a more welcome sound than I might care to admit.

Stepping across the porch, I unlocked the door and switched on the light. In my peripheral vision I noticed that just next to where the dog had been sitting lay an unmarked envelope which, in a single motion, I stooped down, picked up, and slipped in my coat pocket, all the while praying Meghan hadn't noticed. The crunch of her footfalls on the peastone gravel sounded like an old man rhythmically rasping, maybe coughing out his death rattle or else softly chuckling.

"What are you doing out here in your coat?" she asked with a smile as she climbed the couple of porch steps and gave me a kiss.

"Me? Oh, that dog was back here barking and I came out to shoo him off."

"Well, he's becoming a nuisance," she said, as she stepped inside and removed her mackintosh. "Maybe we ought to ask around, see if any of the neighbors knows his owner. We certainly don't want him prowling around here when the baby comes."

I remained on the porch for a moment, gazing at the fully darkened scape outside, whose shapes and borders were now dulled by nightfall.

"You coming inside? You're letting in all the cold."

"Sure, sorry," I said, before backing inside and bolting the door. I agreed with her about the dog, and promised I would make some enquiries the next day.

Sometimes I wondered why Slader didn't simply go to the police or, even worse, to Meghan directly, make his bold accusations, and be done with it. This was my nightmare scenario, naturally, and, as such, one I pictured the man would find most appealing. But the only profit from that course of action was revenge, not money, and Slader, for all the complexities of the relationship I sensed he had with Adam Diehl, was motivated principally by filthy lucre, the god-almighty buck. It was a pretty conventional shortcoming, I understood, for such an otherwise twisted psyche.

His letter, which I read downstairs after Meghan had gone to bed, proposed—well, truth to tell, demanded—a meeting. All rather civilized, he wanted to have a late lunch at the hotel restaurant where he had been staying, coincidentally on Henry Street right near the center of the village. The letter, this time dispensing with Yeats's holograph and written in the block letters of any schoolboy, went on to say,

> *This shouldn't present too much of a difficulty for you, I wouldn't think, as it is just across the street from your place of employment. Yes, I chose it for just that reason. I must tell you how much I admire your punctuality com-ing to and going from work. The underlying responsibility inherent in showing up on time gives me hope that you and I will be able to find a solution to our problems and stick to that solution as if it was law. Because it must be, you know.*

For all that he was a raving psycho, I couldn't help but respect his persistence and audacity. And, bizarre as it may sound, I climbed upstairs to join my wife in bed with a weight lifted off my shoulders. Settling my head on the pillow, I was grateful that some end was possibly in sight, and that despite Slader's verbal swagger and menacing stunts with the poor half-wit dog it seemed possible he wanted to strike a civilized business deal with me. Why meet in an elegant old hotel restaurant if he had another script in mind? Dark alleys, fog-festooned graveyards, dingy dripping grottoes—these were the standard locales for violent encounters, gothic sites that mirrored the gloomy minds of those who haunted them. Not a pretty wall-papered room with silver cutlery clinking against china plates and smiling servers ticking off the daily specials. What was more, having already guessed what he was likely to propose, or at least some semblance of it given what he asked for last time, and figured what my counterproposal might be, I slept well that night, no bad dreams, and woke up more refreshed than I had been in months.

Typical of his methods, he hadn't provided me with instructions how I might go about agreeing to the meeting, which he had called for the next afternoon. I took it upon myself to leave a note for him at the front desk of the hotel, stating that I would be there at three as proposed. It was a late hour for lunch, but I assumed he wanted to get together at a time when the dining room would be more or less vacant, a quiet public place to have a quiet private talk. Although there was no Henry Slader registered at the hotel, I described him to the manager who said, "Oh, yes, Mr. Henry Doyle, I believe you mean," to which I smiled a little and handed him the envelope, saying, "That's him. Could you make sure he gets this?" I walked across the street and down the few doors to Eccles's shop, convinced that Slader-Doyle's eyes were on my back. Fortunately, I didn't give in to my sarcastic juvenile temptation to turn around and wave at the upper windows of the hotel. My self-conscious gait, its strides too long and confident for the short distance, and the unhappy butterflies fluttering in my gut, must have been a sight. I couldn't open and shut the front door of the shop quickly enough.

Work was slow. Tourist season was over as the cold had really begun to settle over Kenmare. The hours dragged. Eccles had no jobs for me on the press, so I did some inventorying, moved our selection of Christmas cards to the front racks, and helped with getting holiday decorations arranged in the shop windows, the usual pine boughs and strings of white electric lights. This was the time, I was told, when we mostly sold stocking stuffers, diaries for people to write their most secret thoughts in, funny pencils and leprechaun gag erasers, yes, not to mention decorative paper and ribbons of all colors to wrap them in. I kept glancing out the window into the street involuntarily, thinking I might see Slader there, but as the daylight faded early—we were nearing the first day of winter—faces became obscured, even though the windows of shops, pubs, and other businesses up and down the street were cheerfully aglow.

Off and on throughout the afternoon and into the drear evening—Meghan was feeling a little under the weather, so I made us a simple dinner of broth and an omelette—I found myself going over the events that had shaped and reshaped my life these past years. At the forefront of my mind was Henry Slader. In particular I found myself wondering why he had developed an animus toward me that truly felt like visceral hatred. Of course, we had tangled, albeit unintentionally to some degree, on crossed business matters. Two forgers interested in the same authors, furtively competing in the same small market, and forced by specialization to share some of the same contacts, were never destined to become fast friends. Be that as it may, I found it inexplicable why Slader would spend such time and effort, not to mention money—*The Winding Stair* was not a cheap book; flights to Ireland weren't free—in an attempt to frighten me, bully me, threaten me. The punishment did not seem to fit the crime.

While absentmindedly clearing the table, Meghan having gone to the living room to read and rest, I found myself wondering whether there wasn't even more to Henry Slader's connection with Adam than I had previously imagined. Had Adam been a source of far more money for Slader than I'd imagined, the police would have had reason to question him twice, would they not? That might at least begin to explain his current behavior. And if the invoice I discovered in Montauk was only the tip of the proverbial, now melting iceberg, then he would be right to believe—since he seemed convinced I had killed Adam—that I had stolen more from him than just the Baskerville forgery. Small comfort that I was reminded of the nineteenth-century debates in British Parliament about whether forgery itself could be defined as theft and therefore the appropriateness, or not, of the death penalty as punishment. Today I found myself siding with Charles Bowdler, who argued in 1818 that "men may as well employ themselves in pelting the sun with snow-balls, as in raising arguments to defend the taking of life for the offence of Forgery." I had to wonder where Slader, who, unlike me, had probably never read Bowdler's treatise *On the Punishment of Death, in the Case of Forgery*, would stand on the matter. If he considered me not just a murderer but, in some ways worse by his lights, a thief, a larcenist unwittingly bent on putting him the poorhouse, what then?

I lied to Meghan that night, which I believed was sometimes a justifiable and even necessary sin. She had found a modicum of peace in her life after her brother's death. Withholding certain things that would hurt her or cause her undue worry was not only fair but wise. With this in mind I mentioned to her that Eccles wanted me to meet with some people tomorrow afternoon around three to discuss the possibility of our combining efforts to start a small press.

"Really? That's wonderful," she said.

"Well, very preliminary and it might not happen," I invented, immediately wanting to backpedal.

"What sorts of things would you publish?"

"Just chapbooks, I think, limited editions on nice laid stock and stitch-sewn into heavy paper bindings. Local authors, mostly poets I guess, who would underwrite the books. I don't know. It's all just come up."

I wasn't thinking clearly. Why invent such a complicated ruse to buy myself an hour or two with Slader? When Meghan exclaimed, "What a wonderful idea," my heart, already leaden, sank further.

"Well, mind you," I said, voice lowered as if by doing so lessened the reality of the project I had fashioned out of pure fantasy, "this could be totally pie in the sky."

"Either way, I like it. Can't wait to hear how the meeting goes."

"I'll let you know," I said, relieved she went up to bed soon after.

The word *seek-sorrow* returned to me, like an acidic reflux in my throat, as I finished washing and drying the dishes. At least, I assumed, while I slowly climbed the stairs to join Meghan in bed, as tardy and tentative as some geriatric, that Slader and his hound would not be up to their miserable dramatics tonight. My path back out of that small deception was easy enough to forge. The meeting went poorly, alas. The project was stillborn.

Just after sunrise, a lissome creamy fog reclining in the treetops of the forest out the window, I dressed and went to work on the early side to avoid further discussing and thereby perpetuation of my preposterous lie. Still not feeling well, although she was long past her days of morning sickness, Meghan decided to spend the day home in bed. Having never before been absent from work at the bookshop, she figured this once the proprietor could manage without her. Naturally, wanting her as far from Kenmare village as possible, I concurred, palming her forehead and commenting she was a little warm and clammy which, as it happened, she was. Irish weather finally caught up to you, I suggested.

"Good luck with your meeting," were her last words after I kissed her goodbye, having brought her soda bread, butter and jam, and a pot of cinnamon spice tea on a tray.

After marking my anxious time at the stationer's— I distractedly undercharged one woman then over-charged the next—I told my boss I needed to leave early to meet a good friend from America for a late lunch, yet another lie, and left for the day, walking across the street to the hotel restaurant. Slader wasn't there even though it was a little after three and, so far as I knew, all he had to do was waltz down the stairs from his room. I ordered a pint. But as the girl left to get my drink, I changed my mind, and asked her instead for a double Connemara neat.

He made me wait a very long half an hour while I began to worry that he had taken it upon himself, while situating me here for our supposed meeting, to go out to the cottage and present his case against me to Meghan. As my second double arrived—irony is its own god—so did he.

"Sorry I'm late," Slader said.

How can I describe my feelings as I sat there, watch-ing him order a Jameson, for the first time looking closely, minutely even, at this man who had caused me so much grief and trouble, and to whom I myself had been, it seemed undeniably, such a scourge?

"So, here we are," he interrupted my thought, or dis-placed it.

"Here we are."

Looking across the table, I couldn't help but admire how civilized the man was with his prominent cheekbones, his dark eyes serious as a scholar's, his black wide wale corduroy jacket tailored but comfortable, his graceful hands and fingers markedly veined and white as gypsum. He was both more elegant and physically sturdier, more robust I suppose one could say, than I remembered him during our cat-and-mouse Armory encounter and the brief meeting we had afterward. What struck me most, and it was such a quicksilver thought that raced across my consciousness it hardly seemed real, was that I saw in Henry Slader, this visible, visceral Slader, someone who in an ideal world I ought to have been able to talk to honestly about what we most loved. If there was anyone alive with whom I could have an in-depth, sophisticated dialogue about forgery it would be this fellow artist seated but a few feet away from me. Absurd, momentary lunacy, I knew, rebuking myself as I lifted my glass in a toast, saying, "*Sláinte.*"

"*Sláinte,*" he echoed.

We looked at each other wordlessly for a few moments before he asked, coolly, "You hungry?" setting his glass back down and glancing at the paper menu that, as it happened, Eccles and I had printed at the shop earlier in the week.

"If you are, yes. If not, not," I said, watching Slader casually peruse his menu. "But are we really here to eat food?"

"Oh, I don't see why not. Myself, I'm famished. Order something nice, the fish here is excellent—"

"I'm aware."

"Besides, lunch is on me since you were kind enough to take the time," he continued, offering up an exquisitely belligerent smile as he waved our waitress, the only other person in the room, over to our table and asked her what was the catch of the day. When she left with two identical orders—I had neither an appetite nor much interest in the touted mackerel or any other fish netted out in Kenmare Bay that day—he picked up just where he had left off. "Although I suppose it's safe to say that you're not here because you really want to be. So maybe 'nice enough to take the time' isn't exactly right. Doesn't matter. I'm glad you came. It's important we figure a few things out."

Grateful he wanted to get down to whatever was on his agenda sooner rather than later, I said, "Couldn't agree more. Look, before you tell me what you have in mind, I'd like to say something."

"We're here to talk. Go for it."

"For whatever it's worth, and it probably isn't worth much at this point, I'm sorry about that Baskerville business. I shouldn't have copied it. I shouldn't have sold it."

Slader ran the tip of his index finger around the rim of his whiskey glass, staring me in the eye. "No, you shouldn't have, should you. But it's not that your apology isn't worth much. It's that it's not worth enough."

"Well, I'll definitely give you the money that Atticus gave me."

"That is a foregone conclusion."

We said nothing as the waitress returned to the table with our soups, asked if we wanted another round—we did, but switched to wine—and left.

"Fair enough," I said.

"Let's get something straight right at the outset. I didn't come to this picturesque little backwater to eat mackerel, drink wine, and be fair. Any chances of my being fair to you are long since gone. They were gone longer ago than you seem to understand."

"All right," I said, quietly, as the girl returned with our bottle, opened it, and poured. "What's your idea of not being fair? If I can manage it, I will."

He waited for her to leave before saying, "Oh, you'll manage."

Longer ago than I seemed to understand. My musings about Adam Diehl returned, and I flirted with asking Slader in so many words how integrated into his life and business Adam had been. But then I remembered a line Orson Welles said in my favorite of his films, about art forgers, that went something like, "We hanky-panky men have always been with you." What it meant to me at that moment was that, Adam Diehl's death aside, the very idea of fairness or unfairness was meaningless to the likes of me and Henry Slader, and that our kind has always been around and always will be. Slader and I were merely two iterations of a grand and dirty tradition. We both were forgers as well as forgeries— we pretended to be real men, sophisticated, educated, entrepreneurial gentlemen, men who got away with what we set our minds to get away with. But much as it pained me to admit it to myself, we were only the shadows of men of true substance. I didn't so much feel sorry for the likes of us as I found us vaguely amusing. In my nervousness I'd had too much to drink, granted, but the swirl of ideas made perfect sense to me. Fleetingly, I felt a kinship with this fellow lost soul I recognized as a complex colleague more than a simple adversary.

"Penny for your thoughts," Slader said, bringing me back to the present reality.

"Real penny or counterfeit?" I asked.

"You're right," he said, not laughing. "Doesn't matter."

"Can we stop playing around and get to what it is you want from me?"

"Here's what I want," lightly tapping out the syllables on the table for emphasis. "As just now agreed, you give me the money Atticus Moore paid you for your bowdlerized copy of the Baskerville work."

"You mean the perfected copy of your Baskerville work."

"Let me remind you, you're not in a position of power here. Not if you want your little life with your little wife to go on in its current state of conjugal bliss. Next, I need another half million, as well."

"Punitive damages?" I smirked.

"No, those come in a minute. The half million's in lost revenues."

"How have I possibly cost you lost revenues?" I asked, sobering up, seeing that those eyes that had earlier impressed me were now as cold and implacable as those of any natural predator.

"Are you really more dense than the police? Do I have to spell it out to you? When you killed my friend, my partner and protégé, your brother-in-law—"

"He wasn't my brother-in-law and I didn't kill him."

"—in doing so, you killed my best connections through him. And don't insult us both by denying you killed him."

"How do you know I killed him? Based on what evidence?" Sensing my right hand quiver, I smoothly moved it from the table to my lap.

"I didn't know, I guessed. Based on what he told me about you. He didn't like you, he feared you. And when you paid me, then I knew."

"You know absolutely nothing. And if you're so god-damned knowledgeable about all this, Aristotle, why didn't you turn me in?"

Slader leaned forward, his face pulled into a mask of fury as immense as it was contained. "That's a rude and complicated question, but the simple answer is that it wouldn't serve my purposes." His voice never rose in pitch or volume. He leaned back in his chair, offered a mercurial smile, picked up his spoon, and took a sip of his soup.

I was breathless. As I absorbed his words, it dawned on me that Adam Diehl seemed not to have been a forger at all. Had I ever personally witnessed him mak-ing a forgery or discussing the art of forgery? I had not. Did I have hard evidence of his trafficking in forgeries, including that ill-fated Baskerville archive he'd gotten from Slader then sold to Atticus, who in turn sold it to me? Yes, I had. But did I know with absolute certainty that he had done the work himself? I did not. Those ink pots discovered at the crime scene, were they actually his own—those, as Slader seemed to have intimated, of a novice—or were they used by a visiting Slader come to Montauk to do a little work on some volumes Diehl had acquired? Was that copy of Yeats's *Collected Poems* one of Slader's misfires, a discard forgery that cost Diehl little or nothing to give to his sister, whom he figured would never know the difference one way or the other?

Or might it have been Adam's hand after all, but the early scrawl of an unpromising student rather than a sloppy professional? All questions that seemed to have the faint, wretched outlines of answers.

I should have been appalled and maybe terrified, but instead I was awestruck. I would probably never know the truth unless Slader could somehow be maneuvered into confirming or denying that Adam Diehl had died a meaningless death, a wrongful death in the most fruitless of ways. Either way, there was no going back to reattach his hands or unbludgeon his head, bring him back to his rather barren life and hope that, going forward, he might hitch his wagon to a star instead of a black hole.

"Let me get this straight," I said, regathering my focus and fully aware of my impertinence. "You and Adam Diehl worked together?"

Slader ignored me. "So, half a million. Make it six hundred thousand with interest and to cover collection costs. The Baskerville money. And most important, going forward, seeing as we both have a number of breadwinner years left to live—"

"Unless you and your patsy dog kill me," I interrupted. "Tell me, where did you find him, Slader? Poor thing chewing on bloody gloves—"

"You're going to start doing what you do best again. I'll provide you with what's needed, and everything will be fine."

So that was how my debt was to be paid. Adam, who was chronically indebted to Meghan and, it was now becoming clear, Slader—a liability that was the product of his insatiable collecting, with large sums of money going out and little or no money coming in—was forced to earn his way out of the hole as Slader's fence. And now, according to Slader's plan, I was to become, as it were, his hired hand. For a rare instant, I felt a twinge of regret that my life had fledged and taken wing in the particular way it did. Whether by will or habit or the ineffable stamp of personality, this unwonted moment passed as quickly as it had arrived. And good riddance. Regret is for the ruined, the bereft, the fallen, and I was none of those. Yet what expectant parent wouldn't worry over the threat of a stirring beast, unless said beast was safely tucked into the pages of a nursery rhyme book?

The fish arrived. Our waitress asked if we were going to have any more of the soup. We both shook our heads. When she removed the bowls, I really hoped she would eat mine back in the kitchen, so thin she was.

"Sorry, but the answer's no," I said.

"You're not in a position to say no."

"I'm sitting here telling you the answer is no. Do you want me to stand and say it? Would that be a better position? Look, Slader, while I might enjoy being your elf, I'm finished with forgery. I swore to Meghan, my wife—"

"I know her name, man."

"—that I would never do it again, and I won't."

Slader surprised me when he laughed. Not because he did laugh. That much might be expected, I supposed. But because his laughter conveyed sincere amusement, with no notes of intimidation or sarcasm or ridicule or contempt. Slader simply found what I had said to be comical. He understood, I realized, what Welles did— once a forger, always a forger, always a hanky-panky man.

I saw no need to repeat myself yet again. That sort of line, the emphatic repetition with back of the wrist set against the brow, was for heroines in grocery-store bodice rippers. Would that we were, yet when Slader stopped with his hilarity, his face clouded over with a cool impassivity. I realized it was the face of a man who had passed most of his life by himself, heedless of others because there generally were no others interacting with him, anyway. Unguarded for just a trice, his former polish, his edgy superiority and genteel machismo, fell away to reveal a face that was, for want of a more nuanced way to phrase it, stupid. Worse, mindless. Slader looked like a thug.

"Let's talk about the press at your shop. I understand it's very old. And that your Mr. Eccles has trays and trays of even older type."

"Leave Eccles alone," I warned him.

"Who said I had any intention of bothering Mr. Eccles? If I can procure the paper and mix the correct ink, could a late-nineteenth-century document, or earlier, be produced on the thing?"

Meghan's prophetic jab that I never consider printing any broadsides by Poe or Byron, or was it Keats, came to mind.

"The answer is, I'm not sure. The more important answer is, I won't do it. And the most important answer as far as we both should be concerned is, I wouldn't know how to do it well enough for either of us to get away with it for long."

"That's my problem, the getting away with it part."

"Listen to me. Atticus has a number of books I consigned to him, amazing stuff from my father's library, which as you know was impeccable. I can simply let you have all the rest of what's left."

Slader wagged several fingers at me. "Already know all that. Impeccable might be what they were before you ornamented them—I looked them over when I was up in Providence a couple times."

I started to speak but Slader interrupted, having anticipated me.

"Don't worry, I didn't say anything since I figured they would be paying your way out of the mess you're in with me, anyway. But that'll cover the six hundred or so and I need more, and so will you. So, you see, I come in peace with a peaceful collaboration in mind."

That sugary characterization of his reasons for wanting to meet with me didn't make me feel a bit more trusting of him. If anything, less so.

"Even if I were willing to get back in the game, I'm too much a novice to be able to guarantee the work would pass muster. Your buyers could be blind as bats, but another one of their senses would betray the work as a fraud—"

Slader opened his mouth to speak, but this time it was I who interrupted him.

"But let me go home and think about it overnight. I acknowledge I owe you money. Owe you even more than that, as you see it."

"Fair enough, but I have a request. I'm asking you not to bring this up with your wife. We both already know what she'd say, so even broaching the subject would be a waste of time. The less she knows about me, the better for everybody's health."

Did Slader just threaten Meghan and me? He did, the bastard. Without even having to head back to the cottage to sleep on his absurd proposal, I knew the answer. There was no way I would be able to cooperate

with this insufferable maniac. A thought flashed by
with meteoric quickness but none of a meteor's burning luminosity—abysmal darkness instead. To wit, it occurred to me that Slader here might want to consider
his own health while he was blithely assigning tasks and
doling out warnings.

"You have my word," I said. "I would never want her
to know, anyway."

Slader smiled and drained his wineglass. "Your word,
my word. They don't amount to much, do they."

"In this case, my word amounts to more than you
know," I said, setting down my napkin and rising from
the table, given there was little left for us sophists to
impart to one another. "Will we meet here in the morning, then?"

"Ten o'clock?"

"See you then," and I turned and headed for the
door, threading my way past tables that were all set and
readied for the dinner crowd.

Slader called out, "You didn't even have a bite of the
mackerel. It's delectable."

I glanced back over my shoulder and saw that he
had carved a piece for himself and had tucked it into
his mouth. As he slowly chewed, his face wore the look
of a gourmet's deep satisfaction, his eyes half-closed in
a kind of sensual, secular ecstasy.

MEGHAN DREW HERSELF UP on one elbow in bed when I came into the room to check on her.

She looked a little paler than usual and her normally lustrous hair was matted and dull in the vesper light. Out the window I could see Venus winking above the highest limbs of the trees, beautiful and totally indifferent to human affairs. "How'd the meeting go?" she asked, after clearing her throat.

"In a minute. First, how are you feeling? Not much better, doesn't look like."

I sat down next to her on the bed and moved my pillow under hers so she could half sit up. Her forehead was no warmer than before but small beads of sweat glistened on her skin. Removing the thermometer from a water glass on the side table, I took her temperature, using the brief silence to collect my thoughts about what and what not to share with her. I wasn't used to Meghan being sick, as she was usually the very picture of health. Back in her old bookshop she had posted a broadside near her desk that quoted the words of another favorite of her poets, Ezra Pound, who had been Yeats's intimate back when Pound was young and aspiring. I could picture that poster as clearly as if it were right here before me. It read in large letters, *The book should be a ball of light in one's hand.* Once, early in our relationship, just about this time of evening after the shop had closed, Meghan and I were sitting across from each other chatting over coffee when I quipped, "You're a ball of light yourself, you know." At that moment I knew without question that I loved her. She came back with a quip of her own, "Like a book, I'll be brighter in your hands," which only strengthened the conviction of my affection.

Here, tonight, knowing I was at a crossroads, I felt that abiding love for her anew, not that it had ever left, not really, even in my saddest, most delirious, deranged hours. Seeing her dim like this, her usual incandescence dulled by what would prove to be a passing flu that didn't adversely affect her pregnancy but just slowed her daily pace a little, I knew that I must do everything within my power to protect her. If that meant becoming a forger again, so be it, I thought. But more likely it meant turning Slader down.

"Your temp is around a hundred, about the same as this morning. Let me bring you some more broth, something to eat?"

"Sure, that would be great," she answered, settling back down into the pillows. "How about the meeting, though? My boss called to see how I was feeling, said he saw you talking with someone at the hotel across from Eccles's this afternoon. So it went well? I've been thinking what a wonderful opportunity it would be for everyone involved."

Struggling to hide from my expression the utter dismay I felt at that moment, I fudged, "Yes, that was one of Eccles's contacts. Look, I can't really tell how it went. Too early to say. One thing, though, is we all agreed to keep it under wraps until we decide to either go ahead with it or not. That way, there'll be less disappointment if it falls through."

"And more excitement when you do announce. Makes sense," she said, not having noticed the pang of regret I felt at lying to her.

Having brought her some supper, I kept Meghan company for a while until she fell asleep again. Quietly as I could, I closed the bedroom door and slipped downstairs into a corner study off the living room, then discreetly shut that door, too. Uncomfortable as the call might be given the things I would have to confess in order to get the soundest advice, I needed to talk to Atticus. I hardly knew what time it was in Providence, my mind aswim, but wasn't overly surprised when he answered. He'd likely have picked up no matter what the hour.

"Always good to hear from my foreign correspondent," he said. "How is all and everything?"

"Most all and everything is fine. Meghan's got a cold, nothing horrendous."

"And you?"

"I'm generally okay."

"You don't sound okay at all," he told me without the slightest pause. Atticus knew me well, I thought, better than nearly anybody. No need to obfuscate, and besides, the whole purpose of this awkward gesture was to seek counsel.

"You remember Henry Slader."

"Of course."

"I don't know how to explain this, but I've got a real problem with him."

"Problem of what kind? He owes you money?"

"No, the other way around. I owe him money and he's flown all the way here to Kenmare to demand I pay."

"Seems pretty extreme," Atticus said. "What did he sell you, a first folio?"

"I wish it was a laughing matter, but I'm going to have to ask you to give him all the rest of the proceeds from whatever's left of the books I consigned you. If you don't mind, I'd rather you paid him directly, as he and I don't get along and I know he trusts you. Is that a problem?"

There was a pause at Atticus's end of the line before he said, "All right. But I'll need to have a letter of authorization from you, if you don't mind."

In all our years of business, he had never asked for such a document before, although we had done millions of dollars of transactions.

"You'll want a final accounting, when the last of the inventory is sold?"

"I suppose so, but it won't make any difference. Slader's due the money whatever the amount, and I would just as soon get this damn monkey off my back."

Atticus's voice shifted into a different register, more grave, even stern. "I don't like the sound of this. A while ago you mentioned that some dealings you had with Slader had gone off track. You care to share what happened?"

If not Atticus, then who could I talk with? Before plunging into what would have to be the partial truth, I hesitated—no way was I going to tell him that there were two copies of that Baskerville archive, one superior to the other but neither of them by Arthur Conan Doyle, son of Mary Foley and the terminal drunkard Charles Altamont Doyle, may they all rest in peace. Further, there was the matter of what Slader felt he held over my head regarding Diehl and why he believed it plausible to blackmail me, none of which I could broach with Atticus. This was dangerous ground I now proposed to traverse, and for a moment I considered backtracking. Then the image of Slader consuming his mackerel with a look of infinite self-satisfaction returned to me, and that settled things.

"I may not be able to answer some of your questions as to the whys and wherefores, Atticus, but the bottom line is, Slader wants me to start forging again."

"That seems easy enough. Just tell him no."

"Not only that," I continued, aware that I skipped right past his rational advice. "He wants me to get involved in print forgery, not the calligraphic stuff."

"But since when do you even know how to print?"

Sensing that Atticus was somehow missing the main point, I said, "I don't really know how to print, obviously. All right, so I've learned a little here in Kenmare working at the shop. I think I mentioned to you we have a lovely old Vandercook and I'm getting to use it more and more. Still, that does not make me a printer."

Almost as if he hadn't been listening to me, Atticus said, "That's really quite a wonderful skill to learn."

What, this was Atticus? I couldn't believe it. "You're sounding like Meghan now," I said. "She's all for it, thinks I should start a small publishing business for local poets and such, but I might add she emphatically doesn't want me even to think about using it to forge anything."

"And Slader, you're saying, does. Interesting."

Here, just here, a strong uneasiness about what I was hearing on the other end of the line began to settle in over me. First, I was sure I had mentioned Eccles's Vandercook proof press to Atticus at Thanksgiving and even recalled him asking if I thought it would be at all practicable for us to letterpress print a ream of new letterhead for his shop on some heavy Crane's paper. "Something I'd use for snail mail correspondence with customers who would be appropriately impressed," he had said, or something to that effect. Maybe he had simply forgotten. No, very likely he had forgotten, but his response to my damned predicament with Slader confounded me. Was it paranoia on my part to think he was sidestepping, like one admiring the pretty scrub flowers that grew on the lip of a volcano while ignoring the orange lava below? I decided to plunge ahead.

"And Slader, I'm saying, does," I echoed, needlessly.

"Well, you know how I feel about it. I hardly need to remind you how I stuck by you when you went through all that hell when you were exposed—"

"And you know I'm forever grateful for that."

"You'd do the same for me any day of the week, I'm sure."

"Of course I would," I said, as was expected.

"Because friends have to stick by friends, even when they may not understand why one or the other has made certain decisions, taken certain steps."

Why was he saying this? I swallowed. "That's how friendship works. But let me remind you, Slader may be your friend. He's not mine."

There was a silence on the line before Atticus said, "I hate to see friends quarrel."

A melancholy ache—how else to describe it?—began to seize my neck and shoulders, as if I had been pummeled there with a truncheon wrapped in dampened newspapers, an old-time method corrupt police used when questioning recalcitrant prisoners when they didn't want any bruises to show on the skin. Ridiculous, I thought. Slader had obviously so upset my purposely narrow and provincial world with his toxic ideas that I now found myself suspecting one of my oldest, most revered friends—one who, as he rightly said, stood by me through my toughest of times.

"Atticus, listen. Bottom line is, I think I may have to go public on this guy if he keeps after me like this. You know I've already paid my dues. And I'm willing to pay him his money. But I have a child coming soon, and Slader's world isn't one I can live or work in anymore."

"You've got to do what's best for you and Meghan," Atticus said. "I know it's a platitude, but platitudes are often the truth."

That made me feel relieved, the old Atticus I had known, serving up warm bromides when a situation called for just such simple fundamental truths. But he went on.

"I wonder what good would come of going public, as you say, on Slader, though. Some things are best kept among colleagues, even enemies sometimes, right?"

Relief abruptly turned to distress. Was Atticus, my gold-standard, arrow-straight friend, playing a Janus game? No, I told myself. It couldn't be. Like mud on polished patent-leather shoes, any accusatory thoughts I felt must have been a desperate attempt to soil him through his association with me and Slader.

Then he said, "Besides, why risk raking up your past again, and maybe bringing a lot of negative attention to you and your family, just when you've gone out of your way to retreat from everything?"

With this I understood our conversation was over. I wasn't speaking with the same Atticus Moore I'd been confident I had spoken with a thousand times before. Any hints of mistrust I felt during the call now solidified into fact—insofar as any fact was real, or anything real was a fact. I thanked my Providence friend, careful to betray none of my mistrust even while sensing that I might never speak to him again, and hung up the phone, shattered.

Most of the night was spent replaying, ad nauseam, my talk with Atticus. Maybe I was being overly suspicious about everything and anything related to Henry Slader. So I tried to reason as I turned on my right side, settled, then rolled onto my left, resettled, before lying on my back. Perhaps I misconstrued Atticus's comments and concerns, I strived but failed to convince myself. Mostly I listened to Meg breathe and cough lightly from time to time, hoping she would feel better in the morning but, selfishly, not quite better enough to go into town with me. When I met with Slader to give him my decision and, while I was at it, a piece of my mind, I didn't need to be squinting out the window in case she herself passed by this time and saw me in the restaurant with this unknown man. Enough pressure sat on my chest as it was, like one of those neolithic stones at the Shrubberies. I couldn't handle a pebble's more.

Daybreak was unusually radiant. Not a cloud confiscated an acre of the sky. The air, when I cracked our window to clear away the stuffiness in the bedroom, was soft and savory. Outside, birdsong rang in the woods, a mockingbird, I believe, or one that loved rehearsing its call over and over. It was as if we had slept through winter and had magically awakened on the first day of spring. For a blessed few minutes, Diehl and Slader and Atticus and every forgery and transgression I had ever been involved with didn't exist, had not happened. I could never remember the word for this half-asleep, half-awake state of being—hypnagogic, was it, or hypnopompic?—but a deep part of me wished I could remain caught in its sweet limbo longer than life allowed.

Meghan was feeling better, as it turned out. Her fever had broken and her appetite returned. She came downstairs in her robe and we had oatmeal together. Still, we agreed, to my great relief, that she ought to stay home one more day.

As I drove into town, the weather held. But my worries about Slader—about how he would respond to my refusal to proceed as his partner, his lackey, or whatever he construed my role as in his harebrained scheme to produce printed nineteenth-century forgeries à la T. J. Wise—threw a thick pall over everything. Eccles was indulgent, giving me another couple of hours off work to meet with my American friend—I told him we'd be saying our farewells, which I rather assumed we would—so after I parked the car, I went straight to the hotel and entered the restaurant. This morning several tables were occupied, two couples and a French family on late-season holiday, I presumed. The same waitress who had served us the day before escorted me to the table that it seemed Slader had booked for us. I ordered a coffee and sat, nervously glancing out the windows that gave onto Henry Street. Since Slader had been half an hour late before—he apparently liked making a dramatic entrance, damned diva—the fact that minutes ticked by without him joining me was more a relief than an annoyance. After a second cup was finished and I waved the girl off when she came by the table with the heavy silver pot, offering me a third, I began to worry. What in the equation of our dialogue had I miscalculated yesterday? Had Slader made some demand or statement I hadn't understood? Not likely, as our exchange was as hard-edged and finite as bones set side by side, this claim a femur, that response a tibia, the whole chain of mutual hatred like some petrified spine of a beast that should never have lived.

My thoughts, such as they were, came to an abrupt close when the waitress showed up at the table again, this time holding a pewter tray with an envelope on it. I couldn't help myself, I had to chuckle at the Jamesian nature of the act, its pure Victorian hubris. Slader was going to communicate to me by handwritten letter, delivered on a platter? If he weren't so insane, I thought, he'd be charming.

> That was a very bad idea to threaten exposing me, very bad. I might have thought you would know better at this point. I offered you what I considered the fairest of terms and it is now clear without us having to talk further that you reject those terms. Too bad. Pity.

I folded the letter—Conan Doyle's hand, by the way—tucked it into my jacket pocket, and asked the girl, who, paid to do so, hovered nearby waiting for further instructions from me, what I owed for the coffee. After paying her several times over what she quoted, I walked straight to the front desk and asked to speak with Mr. Henry Slader, or rather Henry Doyle, who was a guest here, and was told Mr. Doyle had checked out earlier this morning.

"Did he leave any messages? I was supposed to have breakfast with him."

"No, sir. None that I see."

Knowing I was wasting our time, I asked the manager if he possibly had left contact information or an address where he might have gone.

"None, I'm afraid."

I thanked him, then strode across the street into Eccles's shop, trying to remain cool. As fate would have it—and fate always operated, in my experience, with a most vivid sense of dark humor—that afternoon I ended up printing announcements for a memorial service.

It would have taken very little effort to switch the name of the deceased with my own name. And given the way I felt, it would have made a lot of sense. My worries ran rampant as I went about my repetitive work. I, who thought of myself as being perceptive, even shrewd for the most part, got a harsh comeuppance here. Sure, I had always considered Slader to be suspect at best, a devil with whom one needed the traditional long spoon to sup. But about Atticus, I had deluded myself into considering him not just a friend but one of my closest friends in the trade. Busy forgiving myself any sins I committed against him, I somehow lost track that such sinning works both ways—transgressors are not exempt from being transgressed against. That idea was like a law of spiritual gravity, and yet I had managed to be blind to it all along.

I was in trouble now and knew it. For one last passing moment, I gave some thought to capitulating to Slader. In many ways, that would be the easiest course of action, although finding free time to work the press without either Eccles or Meghan questioning me would be difficult. It was true that some of Mr. Eccles's wooden type-cases held fonts that were punched in Irish and English type foundries at least a century ago, perhaps longer, and they would be ideal to use for the time period Slader had mentioned. And if he was providing the text, the paper, the ink, as well as offering to take the materials to market, my exposure and therefore my legal down-side was limited, or so I told myself. The real problem was that I had made my wife a promise and just this once believed I ought to keep it, since what kind of a father would I become if I risked my son's or daughter's chances at a normal life, by which I mean a life in which their father wasn't cooling his heels in prison? Besides, and this was the clincher I had to admit even to myself, my heart was not in it. My onetime love of the visceral act—I would sometimes find myself physically aroused when my hand, my pen, my paper were coordinating so perfectly that a kind of calligraphic, pornographic ballet took place before my eyes—had diminished. And just as feverish love inevitably cools, since otherwise lovers would never survive their own passionate fires, so did my obsession.

As I locked the shop and made my way up the street to where I'd parked our car, I knew it was over. An essen-tial and defining phase in my life was finished, gone, not to be rekindled or resurrected. Oddly, I felt freer than

I had in years. Yes, I was worried about consequences, to be sure. But liberated. How I wished I could rush upstairs when I got home and tell Meghan that what she had always hoped for had finally come true. But she wouldn't understand, since she'd believed all along that the poisonous worm that lived in my heart had been extracted and killed for the vermin it was. I didn't want to explain that though it had been largely dormant, the monster still awoke now and then from hibernation and gnawed away at me, and perished at last only this afternoon. Strange that sometimes we must keep secrets that ought to be cried out from the mountaintops.

MEGHAN JOINED ME FOR DINNER downstairs in front of the fireplace, where a peat brick softly crackled. I did my best to keep that warm feeling of liberation going, but as with all good things it soon enough faded. What I wanted more than anything was to sleep. My weariness over what had transpired since Slader's unwelcome arrival in Kenmare had taken its toll. Sleep, a nice long dreamless sleep, was the sole cure for my fatigue, I knew. After setting our dirty dishes in the kitchen sink—they could wait until morning to be washed—we climbed up to the bedroom, changed out of our clothes, and slipped under the blankets. Outside the window, a cloud cover must have blanketed the sky, as I saw neither moon nor planets nor stars. I fell into a deep slumber, my body relaxing as I lay on my back like a newborn, arms at my sides, in a matter of a few tapering minutes.

Next—not even next, abruptly now—I felt a harsh wetness, like broiling fire, as if my right hand by the bed's edge had been thrust into thick scalding water, or else the lively orange lava of that flower-edged volcano I had imagined before. But when was this? How was this happening? Had time collapsed, imploded? I couldn't really answer my questions, barely formulated, because this distracting fire now became icicle cold, or rather *was* at the same time dry-ice blistering frigid. A dream, a nightmare, I thought or supposed, as I gasped awake, choking in air like a drowning man, my eyes blinking in the darkness that seemed to be interrupted by a confined shaft of blue light shining on my body. But a dull crunch and a groan, or harsh guttural growl that came from outside my thoughts, my head, woke me fully and I knew, as my fingers burned again, that I was not dreaming. Two, three more muffled stinging blows to my right hand and I erupted into screams that were almost simultaneously joined by other screams, those of my wife, whose legs were kicking hard beneath the covers as if she were sprinting in place. None of us was speaking in any language.

Instinctive as a trapped beast and with brutal force, I shoved at my assailant—a man was leaning over me, a barbaric grimace on his face faint in the soft sapphire glow of the tiny flashlight clenched in his teeth—but as I did I sensed my right and left hands were different. I must have known what had happened, although I behaved as if my right hand still had all its fingers attached and wasn't mutilated beyond salvation, a stub of meat and bone soaked in blood with which I slugged him, glancing but distracting, before hitting him as hard as I could with my left. Meghan came flying past me in her soon-to-be-bloodied nightgown shouting words, or maybe they weren't actual words but they conveyed her rage and terror, not to mention her courage, because she grabbed the man's forearm before he could bring his—our, yes, our—cleaver down once more.

If I fainted, and Meghan tells me I did, I don't remember much about it. What I do recall before passing out on the floor next to the switch, which I flipped— the grounds around the house were abruptly bathed in light, which shone on the elaborate mess that was our bedroom now—was that I saw the look in Slader's eyes, an ogre caught in the headlights, and understood that not only was he a madman but he had made a terrible mistake. He pushed Meghan aside, dropped the weapon, and, silent as a moth singed by the candle flame, hurried away. The ambulance and local police were at the cottage quickly, Meghan told me the next day when I, not unlike Adam Diehl before me, lay in a hospital bed, although not on death's door or dismembered of my hands. Nor did Slader get very far before the County Kerry authorities took him into custody. Given he was sighted walking into a pub on the outskirts of the village, where he used a public restroom to clean himself up, it would seem that his attack on me had not been all that carefully thought through—although it is true he managed to thwart the security system, to my enduring chagrin and regret, by scaling an old vine slated for pruning along the side of the cottage, cat-burglar style, to a second-story window. Whether it was the blood on his clothes and face or else that wild look in the man's eyes that I myself had seen before I collapsed, the pub owner phoned the authorities at once, and Slader was arrested on the spot.

I did not lose my right hand. Not in its entirety. He managed to cut off my middle three fingers near the knuckle and my pinky at the first joint. Oddly, my thumb remained unharmed. I received excellent care but wonder whether, if we were in Dublin or New York or somewhere with a hospital that had specialists on call who could reattach severed digits, I might have had a hand whose fingers were present and to some degree functional. That wasn't meant to be. Yet as bad as my injuries were, they could have been worse. As Slader would find out later, he hadn't deprived me of the gift of writing. Presumptuous bastard acted on mistaken impulse hoping to end any chances that I might write my name again, or write anyone else's name, by mutilating my right hand. I remembered, while recuperating, a cute mnemonic that one of my grade-school teachers taught us kids way back when we were learning right from left. She said, "If you write with your right, you're left with your left." Slader might have been instructed with that same little ditty. But since I wrote with my left, my right was wrong, as I believe my clever mother phrased it, or my father. Either way, thanks to Slader I would go forward in life as a bit of a grotesque. I would be one of those occasional people noticed on a subway platform or in a post office, awkwardly clutching the newspaper or an envelope, someone we feel a twinge of sorrow for, an ache of inspiration while witnessing their courage, and great gratitude that we weren't encumbered with a similar disability.

Pollock's fresh interest in questioning Slader about the Adam Diehl case came as no surprise to anyone, least of all me and Meghan. I went out of my way not to implicate Atticus Moore, in part because Atticus had nothing to do with Diehl's death. Naturally, pathetically, Slader, who had fingers to point with, pointed his at me, saying I was the one who slaughtered my wife's brother. I have no doubt that while Pollock might have mistrusted me—he had, after all, also dragged me in for questioning more than once—he viewed Slader's claims as convenient and self-serving, not to mention preposterous and, for any foreseeable future, unprovable. Of course, Slader faced more immediate charges and for those he would go to prison, at least for a while.

Had he succeeded in killing me—though I'm not sure he had wanted to take my life—mine would have been a classic copycat murder. However, this is not what Pollock and many others believed, including Meghan and, over time, myself as well, since I preferred their narrative to the one I knew to be closer to the truth. Slader, in other words, had come after me in the same way he had poor Adam Diehl. One couldn't buy better circumstantial evidence than that, and Slader, for all his entrepreneurial instincts, provided it gratis.

Meghan and I went through a rough patch after the assault, my surgeries and rehab aside. I was finally forced to explain to her who Henry Slader was, no easy needle to thread and a task I needed to be careful about since the authorities were operating, like allergens, at the edges of our lives at that time. I gave Meghan as much as was necessary to satisfy her as well as the guards, as the police were called here, and hoped to let it go at that.

"The main thing you need to understand," I said, toward the end of one of our less than pleasant discussions on the subject, "is that Slader came after me not

because I was doing any forgery but because I refused."
Lying in the hospital bed, having finished eating my
paper cup of pineapple sherbert, I readjusted myself so
I could look out the window at the bleak winterscape.
In no mood to argue, I let out a resigned sigh.

"I hate to say it," Meghan responded, ignoring the
plea inherent in my gestures. "Especially with you here
in pain, in the hospital. But there are times I wish I
never heard the word 'forgery.'"

"Meg—"

"Forgery," she spat out the syllables as if they were
rancid shreds of gristle. "It's the ugliest word in the
language."

"Maybe what you're really saying is that you wish
you'd never met me?"

"That's not what I said, and it's not what I mean."

I paused before telling her, "If I could go back and
undo one thing in my life, it would be to tear out the
page in the devil's playbook that stipulated I would be
interested in books, autographs, manuscripts, forgery."

"That's just nonsense. You can have an enormous interest in books and loathe forgery. Most people I know do."

"You can, they can. I couldn't. But," holding up my
bandaged hand for effect, "I've learned to, the hardest
way possible."

I could read from the look—if looks were books—on
her face what she was thinking. No, it was my brother
Adam who learned the hardest way possible. Fortunately, she didn't speak but instead reached out and
cradled my left hand in both of hers. My wife and I
loved each other, I knew, and this was just one more
storm we would weather.

"Let's make a pact," I said. "Let's drop that word from our vocabulary."

"What word?" she asked with as straight a face as she could manage.

I smiled, and deeply hoped I would be able to hold up my end of the pact.

CHRISTMASTIME IS UPON US AGAIN, the holly-jolly season that New York excels at celebrating. A fresh snow muffles the city sounds, reminding me of a delightful moment in my childhood when my father pulled me along in a sled down the middle of our unplowed, snowbound street. Adorable Nicole is five now, my life's joy and, along with Meghan, my reason to keep on breathing. After the break-in and attack that left me maimed for life, our homey cottage in Kenmare mutated into walls, floors, and windows we no longer recognized. Even the baby's room, so lovingly decorated, was sullied. My security system, obviously a wasted effort to deflect the inevitable, was a bad joke in retrospect. And any sweet luster Eccles's Vandercook once held was now tarnished. After my release from the hospital, Meghan and I realized we could no more live in a crime scene in Kenmare than we could have in Montauk. So it was we returned to the States, where I would continue my rehabilitation, and where, in February as it happened, Meghan gave birth to a healthy girl. We rented a walk-up apartment in the old familiar neighborhood near Tompkins Square, a few short blocks from Meghan's old shop. Our baby daughter was doted on to the exclusion of almost everything else. It was fortunate we still had quite a bit of savings left to support our outsider lifestyle, nor did it hurt that Atticus sent along a sizable cashier's check without an accompanying note but clearly meant to satisfy any debts, real or imaginary, and lock us into a mutually beneficial silence.

Several weeks after we had settled into our new place and after the baby was tucked in and had fallen into her enviably rapt sleep, Meghan and I made love, silently but powerfully, the kind of intercourse that borders on religious communion. After her shuddering orgasm, she whispered to me she loved me and drifted immediately off to sleep. Me, I lay there, my heart slowing, my half-handed arm draped over my wife, hoping to join my family in dreamland. But insomnia got me by the throat, and once more I was captive to my night thoughts. Adam's name had come up during dinner out of the blue, Meghan ruing the fact he had the sweetest niece in the world and what a crime it was that he never got to be her uncle. Just a mention in passing, not a long melancholy dialogue, but emerald-green arsenic to me nonetheless. It was surely that allusion that conjured him up, dead Adam's beggarly ghost, as I turned away from Meghan and looked without focus into our darkened room. Over the years, I had rehearsed what went on the night he was murdered and had grown sick of thinking about it. Were I going to wend my way through it, frame by frame, once again, then this had to be the last time, I told myself. The last time, I demanded of myself.

What had I done? By now the reality—that suspect word again—of the incident was so lodged in the receding past that I misdoubted my version of what happened and can no longer be sure whether or not my imagination has embellished things, erased this or that, revised, emended, amended, and so forth.

Without much aforethought but driven by an ire I cannot fully understand, I recall getting my car out of the garage, a cheap monthly outdoor spot on the West Side with chain-link fences topped by razor wire, telling the indifferent attendant I would bring it back in a few days, needed to get some repairs done. This was not anything unusual. My car, a boxy old Volvo that looked like a Matchbox toy some fond child had pummeled with great enthusiasm into the playground gravel, was dated enough to be very used but not enough to be fancy vintage. Vaguely silver, an inheritance from my father that I didn't drive much but couldn't bring myself to sell, the car needed servicing, and servicing it got at a repair shop out in Sunset Park. I chose the place because it was cash only, under the table, or under the chassis as it were. Had the brakes and transmission checked, too. All was well, but even so I tipped the man who ran the shop, as obviously corrupt a human being as one might ever want to meet, five hundred dollars cash on top of what I owed him for the servicing, asking if he would mind if I left the car for a couple of days at his place.

"Between garages and I don't want to leave it on the street," I explained, a nervous tremor audible behind my obvious falsehood.

He glanced over at the Volvo then turned slowly back to meet my eyes, shrugging as if to say, Who you kidding, man, nobody would want to steal that beater.

"I'll have it out of here in a few days, promise."

After a pause, he asked, "Need to keep it out of sight? That's another five."

"Out of sight would be good. But I may need to use it once while it's here, so I've got to have access."

We discussed details briefly, and our handshake, solemn if idiotic, creditable if corrupt, sealed a pact that meant nothing happened here because, in fact, nothing had. I can still picture his ruddy pockmarked cheeks and handsome sloe expressive eyes. Were he married, which I'm sure he was, he was as unfaithful a husband as ever lowered his trousers.

That night I had a quiet dinner with Meghan. Again, for reasons that elude me, assuming there was anything akin to reason involved in the first place, ours was a memorably lovely meal. We splurged on a bottle of excellent Merlot, shared a T-bone steak with creamed spinach and potatoes au gratin. Back at her place—this was when we used to alternate apartments more often than we did after Adam died—we made love and slept together like two kittens might sleep, ridiculously warm and familiar. In the morning, I was up first and brewed our coffee. Meghan sleepy, Meghan with her red hair and pale full lips, coming from dreamland to life, from slumber to sentience, was a beautiful sight to see. I have no words for the wave of devotion, of affection and adoration, I felt when watching her wake up.

Our talk that morning was no different from any other morning.

"What are you up to today?" I asked.

"Workaday workday," she answered. "Nothing special. You?"

"Same by me," I lied.

"See you later?" she asked.

"You bet," I said. "Go out or cook here or what do you want to do?"

"Let's cook in, your place. But just to remind you, I have to appraise a collection downtown so I can't stay over."

I frowned, then said, "So you'd said. Not a problem."

We had, and I would contend still have, a solid and simple relationship. The problem was her brother. Her first-class freeloader, second-rate forger brother—not even worthy of the word "forger" since I now comprehended he was a dilettante scribbler at best and mostly a mere fence, a marionette who danced to Henry Slader's pulled strings—who was doing everything to undermine our relationship.

How did I know this? Letters to her, simply. Adam Diehl, for all his innumerable faults, was a pen-and-paper letter writer, which I admired. And Meghan, no doubt trusting that her boyfriend wouldn't read private correspondence, was never one to hide them from prying eyes, my eyes. This would have been a few weeks before my car needed its spurious repairs.

Maggie, thanks for the five hundred to get the gas and electric co & another creditor off my back. You're the best sister ever. Hope your shop is doing great. In a rush here but can I ask you a question? I don't have the guts to ask you in person, especially because I know how much you like him, but do you totally trust this guy you're dating? You sure he's on the up and up? I'm trying to look out

for you, okay. Bunch of people respect and admire him,
but a friend of mine thinks otherwise. I don't know. Just
wondering. Love, Adam

That friend was Henry Slader, as far as I am concerned, my reputation being what it otherwise was at
the time. Not a single rare book dealer ever suspected
me, or if they did, they sold what I had sold them knowing I guaranteed my materials and accepted returns
for a full refund, no questions asked. The book trade
was, as with any other business, one in which reputation meant everything. World affairs have always been
implemented on similar lines. A diplomatic handshake
might mean averting a war.

No, I never liked this Adam. But now he was in danger, not to mince words. He not only threatened me
with losing the sole woman aside from my mother who
loved me and whom I loved, too, my darling Meghan.
What was more, this hapless remora with his suspect
signatures and idiotic letters that brought the cops to
my door, or so I believed, threatened my first love and
livelihood, my forgery. Hate was not strong enough a
word to characterize how I felt. Disgust, loathing, contempt, just hand me a thesaurus and watch me fill pages
with vile synonyms to describe Adam Diehl, doomed
neophyte. And he had no idea of the animus I felt toward him.

On the fatal night, as the dime detective novel
phrase has it, after Meghan left my apartment around
ten to head back to hers, I dressed, telephoned her as
usual to make sure she got home safely, and left. Making sure none of my neighbors were out and about in
the hall—I would have abandoned my project had I

run into anyone I knew—I grabbed the subway out to Sunset Park. Feigning exhaustion, I dropped my head forward, chin on chest, to partly obscure fellow passengers' view of my face. Watchman's cap and hands stuffed inside my coat pockets helped further to camouflage me, not that anybody was looking. My repair shop man was good to his word, a key to the garage hidden where he said it would be. The neighborhood was dead and I slipped into the night, certain of not being seen.

Every hour was a dream when I drove out. Every minute was like an unconsciousness so blank and empty of imagery and visual content and of sound too, though there must have been screaming, no not screaming, not a sound at all but an audible whump when I hit him from behind with a hard object, a rolling pin that sufficed to stun him as he sat at his desk unaware an intruder had entered the cottage. I wanted to extract one hand but didn't know which was his writing hand, and so I used his cleaver—Meghan's and his parents had outfitted their kitchen beautifully, being amateur chefs themselves, inspiring my girlfriend to collect and disseminate cookbooks—to take away both. As a longtime student of criminal behavior from the mysteries my father owned by the hundreds, I was of course wearing gloves and disposable shoe covers, and went about my business swiftly and as silently as possible, leaving the cottage under dark of night. Pure dumb luck that a light snowfall had just started coming down after I got to my car, with bloodied gloves and bloodier hands in the thick plastic bag I'd brought for the purpose. I arrived back well before daybreak, having replaced the car at the repair shop and returned home, showered and waited for the phone call from Meghan. As for the hands, they were easy enough to dismember, joint by joint, bone by bone, and wrap individually in tissue before flushing each piece down the toilet.

That Diehl had managed to fashion makeshift bandages from dish towels, I suppose by using his teeth and stumps, so he didn't bleed to death, was unnerving if impressive. Even if he had lived, though, he wouldn't have been able reliably to accuse me of the attack since he never set eyes on me. For all intents and purposes, I was never there. By moving wildly about, as I picture it, in a state of semiconscious panic fueled by the adrenaline of a man fighting death, stumbling through the disarray of books on the floor, knocking furniture over before passing out again, he managed to confuse a crime scene that the authorities would, as fortune darkly shined, themselves further deface, further botch.

The phone soon rang. Bereft, she was in Tompkins Square, schoolchildren shouting with glee in the background. My first words to her, after hearing what had happened, were, "Where is he now?" knowing full well that I stood at the beginning of a journey in which the less I knew about Adam Diehl, the more I learned to push him out of my consciousness, the better off I would be. Meghan's dying brother was anathema to me. Having stood between me and what I most cherished, he brought on his own little apocalypse, and there was nothing I could have done to prevent his pitiful outcome.

That was in the dead middle of winter whereas today we find ourselves at the solstice, with a gentle snowfall starting up in the bluish late-afternoon light. As I sit here alone at the kitchen table in our East Village apartment while Meghan and Nicole are up at Rocke-feller Center visiting the big Christmas tree on display there and watching the ice skaters do their scratch spins and figure eights, out of the blue I remember that night when I couldn't sleep, and when I recapitulated Diehl's final days and hours as best I could, with recollections as aligned with the truth as a forger's faulty memory al-lowed. I am relieved I kept my promise to myself not to ponder those dark times any further. While I know that the refusal to think about a wicked act does not absolve one, it does carry the benefit of release, of liberation, and for that I am grateful.

When Meghan and Nicole get home, which ought to be pretty soon, I plan on getting our girl warmed up with some hot cocoa before leading one of our regu-lar father-daughter calligraphy lessons, much the same as her namesake grandmother used to do with me. A shame she will never meet her grandmother, study the crafting of letters and flow of words with her, who was a far superior teacher than I will ever be. Even more's the pity, since young Nicole is—and I posit this not as a dad but an objective expert—bursting with talent. She has a natural aptitude, an unpolished genius, if you will, with pen and paper. I remember my mother being awed by the concentric circles I drew when I was Nicole's age or even a bit older, but they couldn't have been as per-fectly drawn as my daughter's. And she makes them over and over as if it were as simple as breathing in and breathing out. For her sixteenth birthday, I plan on giving her the Arthur Conan Doyle pen that I myself inherited, passing it along to a third generation in our family, a talisman for her to preserve just as her father has and his father did before him.

As for what she will do one day with her calligraphic skills, I cannot say. Perhaps she will become a painter or a set designer, or maybe she'll end up doing something altogether different. Even if the dreams she pursues when she grows up have nothing to do with the act and art of writing, someone, possibly a future best friend or lover or even spouse, will notice the grace of her script on a restaurant bill or mundane shopping list, and comment, "Hey, Nicole, you have the most beautiful handwriting I've ever seen." And just maybe, if my wrathful shadows don't catch up with me and devour the one who got away, she will say with conspicuous pride, "My father taught me when I was young." She will think of me then, a man who now must forever be quietly glancing over his shoulder, with unreserved love in her heart.

ACKNOWLEDGMENTS

Over the years in which I have been involved with the rare book community, both as a bookseller in my twenties and later as a collector, I became friends with more book dealers, special collection librarians, and fellow bibliophiles than I can possibly tally. Richard Schwarz of Stage House II Books in Boulder, Colorado, particularly inspired my earliest love of the field. I owe these book people a debt of gratitude for all I learned from them. It is important for me to state, emphatically, that most booksellers and collectors are noteworthy for their honesty, intellectual vigor, great wit, and wisdom, and have never made the dark journey that some depicted in this novel have taken.

Three respected bookmen in particular, Nicholas Basbanes, Tom Congalton, and James Jaffe, I want to thank for taking time to read the manuscript and offer their expert opinions on the complex world of rare books and manuscripts. I also want to thank Grove Atlantic's Morgan Entrekin, Peter Blackstock, Deb Seager, and Allison Malecha for their belief in this book from the beginning. My friends Douglas Moore, Nicole Nyhan, Eimear Ryan, Hy Abady, Thomas Johnson, and Peter Straub offered thoughtful comments about my manuscript in progress, as did Henry Dunow, who is not only a superlative agent but as serious and sharp a reader as I have ever been privileged to work with. Heartfelt appreciation to all. As for Cara Schlesinger and my editor, Otto Penzler, my gratitude to them for their support in different ways, my thanks for their inspiration, is beyond expression.